AN ANTHOLOGY

"Your manuscript was brought to our attention at the latest Editorial Board meeting when we discussed the potential of its publication. Having read all the reports and taken note of the Editors' opinions we can confidently state that your submission was found to be a most fulfilling and immersive read. A visceral and poignant collection of writings that is sure to resonate with the target audience. The Board was keen to comment on how your work is an alternative piece that puts the author's talent on full display, pushing the boundaries of the genre. Each writing is unique and well-written, and it is felt the work would have a place in the market. Ultimately it is felt to be a worthy addition to the genre. "...

An Anthology

*A Collection of Memoirs, Flash Fiction,
Short Stories, Poems, Travelogues*

❖ ❖ ❖

UTPAL BARUA

© Utpal Barua, 2021
All rights reserved.
ISBN 979-8773025-7-5-7

Disclaimers

In this Anthology selected names, characters, incidents portrayed in, are fictitious. No identification and actual person (living or deceased), places, buildings are intended to be inferred. Any resemblance to persons living and dead should be plainly apparent where the author provided their real names. The author has taken certain very small liberties which are entirely fictional.

To my mother
Late Tarulata Devi

Contents

❖ ❖ ❖

A village trapped in a time capsule	11
The lady at the helm of a space craft	13
Where is Jessie now?	15
A tribute to Dad	18
The death of a desert princess	22
The price	27
A view through the window at night	29
An encounter with the past	31
George Harrison and his ukulele	39
I am a hero	42
Happy days	43
Reminiscing my college days	45
Revisit to The Grange	51
The aftermath	54
The brave new world	56
The future	58
The goddess of Cu Chi tunnels	59
The unsung hero	63
A quick visit to Manhattan, New York	68
The quest	70
Triptych of "Lockdown"	73
Values of changing time	75
A visit like no other	78
Whispering stones and weeping trees. Angkor Wat	81
Hidden jewels of the Lake District	85

CONTENTS

First Easter	87
A Christmas gift	88
The Kipling stories	91
The Hawley	93
Missing pages	95
The man with a foreign hat	98
Dr Freud and the rabbit	101
The way we were	102
The vigil	107
Après moi le déluge	112
The Bridge of Sighs (*Il Ponte dei Sospiri*)	117
A visit to *La Patria*	121
Snippets from bygone springtime	126
August 2021	128
On a cold winter morning	129
Dinner with my uncle	136
A letter to my parents	138
A cruise holiday with my family	141
Sylvia	145
auld lang syne	146
Déjà vu of a cobbled street	148
A place called home	151
My Ergo chair	154
A virtual reunion of batch 1962	156
Goodbye my sweetheart	159

Acknowledgements

❖ ❖ ❖

Thanks for browsing this little booklet. The idea of writing down my thoughts came to me while I went through a period of transition from being a workaholic to a retired person at the beginning of 2019. After toying with a few ideas like travelling, adventures, gardening, tracking down my old friends, taking up new hobbies, I decided to opt for volunteering for an international charity called Global Vision International (GVI). I went to Kochi in India and one fine morning I reported at the first meeting of my new venture at the age of 73 years. To my surprise, I discovered that I was the only one of male kind in that group (except for the group leader). The group leader asked each one of us to self-introduce and asked to tell the group what inspired us to do volunteering. What I found fascinating was that each one of us had a story to tell, a story of personal vision to make our world an equitable better place for all of mankind. Because of my professional background I worked at a school for young people with physical and mental impairment.

On my return home to England, during that winter, sitting on my own I decided to come out of my 'comfort zone'. I met a group of matured people who nurtured an idea of being a writer. Once a week we used to meet up at our local library in Wells, Somerset, England.

Our mentor offered us prompts, exercises, critical analysis and methods to write and technical advice on how to develop writing skills on a wide variety of genre.

On 6 January 2020 a 23-year-old Chinese student who travelled to York University in the U.K. from his home in Hubei

ACKNOWLEGEMENTS

province in China fell ill with severe "Viral Pneumonia". On 11 January 2020 China reported death of a 61 year old man from similar symptoms of the same disease. Later they named the new disease as Corona Virus infection. By 31 January 2020, the UK confirmed 2 cases of Covid-19 infections. Between 10 April 2020 and 31 March 2021, 39,000 care home residents died of Corona virus infection in the United Kingdom.

The authorities decided to introduce new terminologies "lockdown, isolation, working from home" and many other restrictions to combat the spread of this new vicious illness.

Like many people, now redundant, isolated and bored I decided to write down my recollection of events and vivid experiences accumulated over a period of time. Our classroom work practices changed from physical to virtual writing existence from then on.

I am thankful to my fellow classmates for their support, enthusiasm and advice in compiling my short stories. My special thanks go to Fiona Shillito, for mentoring, guidance, encouragement, empowering to develop our potential and churning out new challenges, come rain or shine week after week.

I want to thank Brian Crowley, Adele Brooks, Christine Tweedy, last but not the least to Lesley McDowell who boosted my self-confidence by reviewing my writings.

My thanks go to my beautiful family for just being there and brightening up the dark moments of my life that followed the Covid-19 disaster when I lost members of my extended family and many of my medical friends who laid their lives fighting Covid-19 infection.

Finally, a big "Thank you" to Josette Prichard of CARRIGBOY, Wells, for all her technical help in producing this book.

A village trapped in a time capsule

Gold Hill Shaftsbury Dorset

❖ ❖ ❖

One of the most amazing iconic advertisement I remember was that of a boy pushing his bike up the hill on a cobbled street to deliver a loaf of bread before freewheeling down to the village bakers. The advert was created by Sir Ridley Scott and music was by Dvořák's New World symphony.

It's now 44 years since that advertisement was produced. The 13-year-old boy, his name, Carl Barlow is now 53 years old. He later joined the Fire Brigade and is now retired. He reported that after 40 years, he recreated the famous feat of pushing the loaded bike up to the top of the hill.

Sir Ridley Scott became a great film director who produced films like *Aliens, Thelma and Louise, Gladiator, Black Hawk Down*. Even at the age of 83 years he is still directing films e.g. *Death on the Nile*.

I have seen a photograph of Sir Ridley Scott, he reminded me of Mark Twain who said:

> Age is an issue of mind over matter
> If you don't mind, it does not matter.

Goldhill, Shaftesbury, Dorset

Mars Rover

The lady at the helm of a space craft

❖ ❖ ❖

You might have heard a lot about the voyage of Spaceship Perseverance's successful journey to Mars on 18 February 2021. The purpose of the $2.7 billion dollars expedition was to install a rover on Mars surface. Rover's 23 cameras recorded landing mechanisms of the final decent of the vehicle, then a "space crane" positioned the rover on the pre-selected spot near the Jezaro crater. I saw the live documentary on television that night at 8.48 pm (British time) and heard a young lady's voice guiding audience with running commentary from NASA's control Centre at Pasadena. She had a confident voice, as if she explained such events many times before. Later I learnt that the commentator was also busy controlling the critical manoeuvres of the space craft while she was talking to her audience. Her job was the Guidance, Navigation and Controls (GM&C) head of operation of NASA Mars 2020 mission leader.

The events during those moments were described as "harrowing, turbulent 11 minutes of hell". Soon after the rover arrived at the Jezaro[1] crater, The PIXL[2] instruments started to measure the chemical make-up of Martian rocks. Scientists previously found traces of methane gas on the Moon surface, a marker of ancient microbial life.

---
[1] Jezaro crater was formerly a lake, where there was probably water, hence life.
[2] Planetary Instrument for X-Ray Lithochemistry spectrometer.

I spent some time thinking about how in my lifetime human ingenuity and endeavours enriched our knowledge, opened up new horizons for the future generations.

When I was a little boy, the Moon was the limit of my imaginations. I heard a story about a man called "Shen Fu" who lived in China. One day he met a beautiful girl on a moon-lit night and fell in love with her instantly. The old man in the moon played a mischief and plotted to bring them together. Soon they got married and they promised to love each other for ever. Unfortunately, the wife died after a short illness, leaving Shen Fu with a broken heart which led him to untimely death drowning in his sorrow.

On 20 July 1969, Apollo 11 left the first human foot print on the surface of the Moon, bringing an end to my romantic illusions.

Now in my sunset years I believe, Mars will be the next destination that mankind will soon colonise. If a lonely warrior called Mars is still waiting for a beautiful Venus (arriving from earth) it will be a happy ending to a long waiting legendary hero.

I hope the young lady (at the base in Pasadena) at the helm of the Jet Propulsion centre will fulfil her dreams of transporting human beings to Mars and returning them back safely to earth.

Her name is "Swati Mohan", meaning the Sweet Star (in Sanskrit). Born in Bangalore, in India.

Where is Jessie now?

❖ ❖ ❖

It was on an autumn day two years ago, I picked up my usual newspaper. There was a story about a young girl who was thrown off when her horse bolted and she sustained serious injuries to her face. She was taken to the city hospital. Doctors were horrified to see the severity of her injuries. Half of her face was hanging by a strip of 1cm skin attached to her chin. For more than five hours, a team of specialists used 3D technology to rebuild her face. She had three titanium plates, 160 stitches. Reconstruction was a great success, only a faint mark was visible on her face.

When I read the story, I thought of Jessie, who was one of my patients many years ago.

After my graduation I was toying with the idea of being a surgeon, although my expertise at that time was rather rudimentary, I managed to get a job as a junior doctor in our Plastic Surgery department. My job included taking full history when patients were admitted as inpatient and I did regular follow-ups, assisted senior doctors during operations, attended clinics and was "on call" as per rota.

Jessie was one of our patients in my ward. I visited her regularly on my evening rounds, when the place was quiet and most patients were watching TV sitting in their lounge. I noticed Jessie did not make many friends, nor she was keen to watch television like other patients. I thought she was lonely and I would sit in her room for a while and chat to give her company. While I looked through her medical history, I noticed Jessie was attending our hospital for many years for facial reconstruction and extensive skin grafts.

One evening I said to Jessie, "I hope you won't mind if I ask you about your burnt face and how it all happened". I tried to be sensitive not to hurt her feelings. After a pause Jessie moved her hands and gently touched her face, then she removed a metallic mask and put it on her side table. That was the first time in my life when I saw, a contorted face totally disfigured with loss of her left eye. What I saw, shocked me, she could clearly see my expressions of aghast on my face. After a short time, she collected her mask and replaced it as before. She looked at me and said "I am not upset with you; you are the only doctor who cared to look at my face since I was admitted into the ward."

Over a period of time, Jessie opened up to tell me her life story. She told me that she was a Londoner by birth. In September 1940, during the Blitz there were many air raids by the Germans in London where Jessie and her family used to live. Not all those bombs detonated when they hit the grounds. Some of them were specifically made with clockwork time-delay mechanisms. They were great menace to Londoners as they were major hazards, particularly for children. One day when she was playing with her friends, a boy saw a bomb and he pulled something out of it, as curiosity got the better of him. Soon after, the bomb went off causing a great explosion, killing the boy and Jessie's friend Jane. This was how her face sustained grave injuries and she lost one of her eyes. She was admitted to hospital and was an inpatient for a long time. Later all the local children were evacuated from London, Jessie was one of them who was sent away to live with strangers. As her elderly hosts were unable to take care of Jessie, she was readmitted to our hospital. Over a period of time Jessie lost touch with her family and she attended our hospital for long term treatment for her injuries. She had been coming to our hospital for the last thirty years mainly for grafting of her damaged skin.

She said, "I am not complaining, all my family and friends are now dead, I am the one who is still alive."

I asked her, "Any thought about the war?"

She said, "War is evil. I spent all my life in isolation mostly on my own".

The following week I told Jessie, "I have finished my training here and will be moving to another town soon, I shall come to see you the day before I leave the hospital".

Jessie said, "You know, over the years I have had many face masks and many doctors. May be one day I shall donate those masks to some medical museum for the sake of posterity. Thanks for your kindness, and for taking time to talk to me".

I left that hospital on the following Monday. Jessie gave me a box of chocolate with a short note. Here is what she wrote to me:

"I know what you wanted to ask me that night, you wanted to know what I got out of my life? There was a time when I wished one day someone would call me 'love', to feel myself loved would have been a nice thing to happen".

It is a long time since I met Jessie. 3D titanium plated facial reconstruction was long way off human imagination.

... I wonder where Jessie is now?

A tribute to Dad

❖ ❖ ❖

"His parents must have loved each other ... in his adulthood, he concluded. After his mother died, he found a letter to her from his father which proved that once they were happy".

Extract from Michel Palin. A Biography
by Jonathon Margolis.

Michael Palin was one of my favourite personalities as a young man 'footloose and fancy-free, living a rapturous life'. Both of us were born in mid-1940s, 5000 miles apart. In his candid expressions (of Michael's thoughts), I sensed similarities of my personal experiences.

Palin describes his father as a bully, a difficult man who made him very unhappy when he was young (see *Michael Palin, A Biography* by Jonathan Margolis).

I recall my father too, had a short fuse, there were very little communication between him and us (his children). Mum was the only intermediary to all the family interactions. We felt dad was remote, the provider, wise and the one who must be obeyed.

In Indian traditions, a father is the "ultimate Guru (teacher)". He commands respect but there is no mention of love.

Today as a curmudgeon, I am trying to understand how our lives and attitudes as a society changed over the last 50 years. Trying not to be judgemental, I looked up a book (written on my father's life) published after his death. This book is based on Dad's personal diaries spreading over 50 years of his lifetime.

My father was born in early 1900 in India. He was the second son of a junior British Indian Government officer. He had 9 siblings in the family. Although the family was rich in land, there was not a lot of cash to support a big family plus dependent relatives and handful of servants with my grandfather's income. What I understand, the family survived in a straitened circumstance.

There was not much attention or love for the children from either of his parents, I can't imagine any of the children ever experiencing a cuddle or a kiss from their parents. Like in every society, life is often influenced by what is happening in the economy and the society they live in. My father's family followed the traditional roles, his father as the head and bread winner and his mother, the home maker. Any naughtiness by their children was dealt with physical punishment as they believed in the saying "spare the rod and spoil the child".

My father was a clever student and grandfather happily paid for his education up to his Master's degree in English and to complete another Master's degree in Law. After his qualifications Dad was offered a position as a lecturer in the first Ladies College established in that part of the world in the English department. But some parents of the students objected to his appointment as he was an unmarried young man. Soon my grandparents found a 16-year-old girl for the newly appointed lecturer son to marry after the astrologers confirmed that their stars were fully compatible with each other. Like millions of Indians, they believed in the phrase "marriages are made in heaven", there was no reason for the couple to know each other before they got married, a life-time commitment preordained in heaven.

After a brief spell as a lecturer Dad decided to join the civil service and over the years achieved the high position of senior Governmental officer. I must confess, I never saw my parents

Mrs Indira Gandhi (*centre*), Prime minister of India FA Ahmed (*second from right*); past president of India Golokeswar Barua; (Dad) (*first from right*), 1966.

arguing or any overt demonstration of affection for each other. They stood together through highs and lows of their long-married life.

After his retirement Dad wrote a number of scholarly books. At the ripe age of 84 years, Dad had a stroke. I went home to see him on receiving the news. I felt sad to find an frail old man unable to help himself, he could not even speak a word, I was unsure if he recognised me, his eldest son.

Soon after, on my return to England, I was informed that my father passed away. After his death, my brother retrieved his old diaries covering fifty years of his life with a view to publish a book.

I was asked to write the preface of that book. To my surprise, I discovered that he recorded a witness account of recent history of Assam during the twilight years of the British colonial rule, at the dawn of a free Nation striving to join the league of other free Nations of the world.

In his writings we rediscovered the long-forgotten important dates and recordings of our family events. It had been a great comfort to all of us, in the family, to know that behind the mask of dour aloofness there was a kind and loving father and husband. The only regret, we had to wait all that long to know our own father.

On reflection of the long gone past, I just came to the conclusion that I had no right to judge my Dad, because I never knew what he had been through in his life. Yes, I have heard stories of hard time, but I didn't feel what he felt deep down in his heart. While rummaging through his files, I found a little endearing note he sent to mum many years ago. I don't know what were the reasons for my ancestor's behaviour which influenced them, neither can I judge their actions, values and ethos of another age using a yard stick of current ideas.

The death of a desert princess

❖ ❖ ❖

Part 1

A few years ago, I visited Bangalore to meet my sister and her family. Bangalore is the epicentre of India's Silicon Valley where one finds technological companies such as ISRO, Infosys, Wipro, Cisco, Oracle and many other international technological organisations. Bangalore is also in the forefront of modern education such as Management, IT, Science, Neurosciences. While I drove around the city, I noticed a signpost, "Karnataka Folklore University", with specific objective of providing knowledge of culture, traditional wisdom and pluralistic connection of human civilisation.

We inherited many myths and fables from our ancestors, passing on from one generation to the next, still fresh in our collective memory. In India people with latest knowledge of technology embrace our past heritage with respect and diligence.

Stories like that thunder and lightning is caused by Jupiter hurling thunderbolts to earth, talking animals, devils and heroes, powers of metamorphosis still continue to ignite the thrill of Indian's imagination. Even today such stories influence young minds with a sense of wonder and inspire to fabricate a magical world, where battles between villains and heroes continue to save our world.

The myths of Echo and Narcissus were born out from the imagination of some story teller who observed human predilections. Echoes are a natural phenomenon but they did

The Witches by Goya.

not know the reasons. Although with our current knowledge we know that echo is a sound repeated because the sound waves are reflected back. Likewise, water is reflective because it is relatively flat like a mirror.

To satisfy human need for an explanation of such a phenomenon our ancestors came up with stories based on prevailing wisdom.

When I was a child, I heard about Marco Polo's adventures in China. In his chronicles he wrote: "The desert spirit can do amazing and incredible things. Even in the daytime their voices can sound of different musical instruments, for these reasons, travellers go in large numbers and stay close to one another. When you approach the town of Lop, you will hear the voices of demons at night. With sounds of all kinds of musical instruments, also of drums and clash of arms". Locals believed those are the voices of demons or spirits trying to distract innocent travellers. Greeks invented many myths, gods and villains to explain

Why the Dunes sing & souls get lost in a desert?

Prologue
Like the Greeks, Indians (Hindus) also created fantasy figures like gods, demi-gods, nymphs, villains and, Heaven, Earth and Hell. Among the Indian myth makers was Vishnu Sharma who compiled a collection of fables called "Panchatantra" (200BC–300BC) where he wrote about talking animals, fairies and heavenly figures. Those stories were translated into 50 foreign languages many centuries ago. It is difficult to identify the origin of many of the myths that adapted to local flavours and passed on all over the world.

The story
This is a story about a Jaminder (Laird) who lived by the Silk Road that connected China to the Middle East and Europe via the

Gobi Desert with his wife and his daughter. According to the local legend, he was a descendant of Alexander the Great who conquered north west India (326BC). When Alexander decided to return home, some of his army settled at the foot hills of the Himalaya. Later they were converted to Islam and the head of the settlers took the title of Khan. Following a family feud, one of the Khan brothers migrated to the north and settled in a little-known town close to the Silk Road. The Khan had a very beautiful little daughter, her name was princess Parisima (face of a fairy). When she grew up, she became a ravishingly beautiful young lady. But there was one drawback, she had a speech impediment. The only person she could talk to was her mother. The Khan who loved his daughter deeply was worried because the Seer (the fortune teller) proclaimed that his daughter was cursed by a Goddess from Heaven.

One day a young man called Timur from a neighbouring clan arrived at the castle and introduced himself as the son of the local Chief of Nomads. Timur said he was sent by his father to inform the Khan that his father was planning to seize Khan's town unless he surrenders to his father's demands.

Khan's chief adviser Kazi (judge) Safiqur Rahman advised arresting the young man and put him in the dungeon. The young man was allowed only to get out from his cell once a day to visit the gardens by the underground river. One day the princess met him in that garden. As soon as Timur saw the beautiful girl, he fell in love with her. He tried to engage the princess into a conversation many a time, but she declined to talk to him again and again. The young man could see twinkles in her eyes when they met and was smitten by her enticing smile.

One day Parisima told her mother, "Mum I made a new friend, he is very nice to me, I too love him a lot".

After a few days her mother gave her a key to the dungeons so that the young couple could meet up more often. When they met, Timur said lovely words of endearment to her, but she never uttered a single word. After a while Timur came to believe the Princess was playing a game and she will never marry the son of highway robber. With a broken heart he decided to escape that night. Before he left, he visited the beautiful garden for the very last time. He left a bunch of Narcissi flowers by the side of the river and disappeared into the desert.

That night, the Princess heard awful noise from the desert. She heard the voice of her lover calling her name from a faraway place. She could hear the clanking of weapons, whinny squeal of the horses, beating of the drums and sounds of bagpipes, trumpets, bugles coming across the desert. It was like an ominous boom that echoed through her heart. She rushed out of her bed and raced through the night looking for her lover.

After three days the Khan sent a rescue team to look for his daughter and the boy Timur. When they arrived at the desert, they found the Princess's horse and saw a vulture spreading his wings over the dead body of the Princess under a hot summer sun.

The gate man guided the rescue team to the local oasis where they found the body of Timur. He was looking at the still waters in the oasis still holding an embroidered handkerchief presented by his lover.

People said the vulture was the soul of Timur and the music was sad songs of those people who perished in the cruel desert.

Selective mutism is a recognised Mental Health Disorder. (First recorded in an Irish Princess).

The price

❖ ❖ ❖

It was like any other day in my surgery. An old couple walked into my room. They were in their mid-70s, obese and looked unwell. That was their second visit to see me following previous week's investigations. The reports were slightly outside 'normal' values, "acceptable for their age", the report concluded.

As a young medic, I was curious to know the reasons for the symptoms they both complained about, they appeared to me as genuine, not of hypochondriac nature.

I decided to explore full medical history of the couple. This is what I learned from their stories:

Mark and Glades were in the Military Service in the mid-1950s. They met at the Maralinga Island in the Pacific Ocean. They were told that they were very lucky to be in that mission as the Island is in warmer climes, surrounded by azure blue seas … just like a paradise. Mark and Gladys met at the kitchen as they both worked in the Catering department, fell in love and later got married when they returned home to England.

Mark said, "We were a group of young people, proud to be part of the British Army experimenting with the most advanced weapons in the world (Britain conducted 12 nuclear bomb tests, H-Bomb included). The pilots were highly skilled, regarded as the 'bravest of the lot' who flew their planes close to the mushroom clouds of nuclear bombs as close as possible, more powerful than the one dropped at Hiroshima and Nagasaki during the WWII. Some of those Airmen were exposed to 12 000 rads of X-Rays in six minutes. Some suffered nose bleeds and vomiting. Those who were very ill, were sent back home to a hero's welcome for their courage and dedication to the nation."

As Mark and Gladys worked in the kitchen, they cooked fresh fish floating off the beach every day for all the staff day after day, enjoying the happiest time of their life.

Latter people realised that exposure to atomic radiation could cause serious health hazards such as Cancer, lung damage, skin lesions, genetic mutations and many other non-specific symptoms and mental health disorder. There has been reports of hereditary birth defects among the children of participants of that mission.

Gladys was right when she said, "It was all for this, all that toil, all for those years of training, what good have we got?"

I just wonder, those who were at the helm of power, do they have a conscience?

A view through the window at night

❖ ❖ ❖

After a long arduous journey, I arrived at my destination, Bangour General Hospital in Scotland. Until that day my experience of the world outside my home town in India was rather limited. I flew through Heathrow Airport, bright lights, multitude of nationalities of passengers, crackling noise of announcements, escalators, sheer expanse of the terminal space was an overwhelming experience. Next, I took my flight to Edinburgh and then the bus to Bangour General Hospital, for another 16 miles. It was a cold damp cloudy day. I was tired, alone, lost in a foreign country and sad.

Bangour hospital was in a remote isolated place with one tiny village shop, a Psychiatric hospital, nothing else. I lived in a Doctor's residence, where I was the only occupant. Soon I realised that almost all the people who worked in the hospital were commuters from Edinburgh. By the time it was 5 o'clock only the 'on call' staff remained.

I spent my time mostly on my own, visiting the library and working as a junior doctor.

One April morning, I woke up to watch snow-flakes fall outside my window for the very first time. Soon a flurry of white flakes spread across the rolling hills beyond the horizon. A ripple of exhilaration, excitement and delight melted my angst away ... I had no one to share my joy. There was not a soul in the vicinity, not a sound, I was all alone.

I missed my family, my friends, my newly-wedded wife ... I missed her a lot. I remember, the window was steaming up. I tried to clear the glass pane with my sleeve ... the steam remained. I realised it was my glasses dampened with tears. I told to myself "I am not crying; a man does not cry".

That night I could not sleep, opened the window, a whiff of cool breeze engulfed my senses laden with pinewood fragrance. I looked at the sky and saw the beauty of a star-studded allure on that night. I saw the twin stars Mizar and Alcor in Ursa major constellation ... I recalled our Wedding night.

The priest pointed to the sky, "Look at those two stars", he said, "They are the symbol of loyalty and of everlasting conjugal love. They go round and round with each other, never apart. In Hinduism Alcor is Arundhati (wife), Mizar is Saint Vasishtha (husband), a married couple in the heavens, your union is now witnessed and blessed by the Gods, your love will never end".

I said to myself ... what a wonderful world.

I smiled; my heartache floated away.

An encounter with the past

❖ ❖ ❖

I have been a regular walker for quite some time. My usual route is along the Cathedral green towards the market place then to the moat towards the old deer park. I am now used to the routine of going out around half past four in the afternoon most week days. Over a period of time I became familiar with faces of local resident walkers and visitors to the town. Last Monday I saw an old couple sitting on a bench silently facing the Chapter house.

I suspected the old couple were visitors. One day when they looked at me, I doffed my hat wished them well and walked along. They were at the same bench at the same time next few days. On the fourth, it might have been the fifth day since I first spoke to them, (thinking about it, it was 13 April, on Easter Friday), I noticed they exchanged a look between them which I found quite disturbing. This was the first time I remember I saw them communicating physically with each other, but the silence prevailed.

I felt there was something odd the way he behaved, I stopped and asked if everything was alright? The old lady pointed her finger towards the Chapter house steps, turned her head towards her husband and said, "Aldhelm, look there is Emily and our grandson Arthur".

I could see no one. Looked again, still there was no one else. I had a spooky feeling about the place, I looked at the old couple once again, she was wearing a tatty old bell-shaped skirt with a high neck long sleeve blouse.

The couple looked tense, sad, agitated, helpless, yet suppressed their anger.

I waited for a while and asked them if I can be of any help, I would be happy to accompany them to their hotel if they wanted. Aldhelm nodded his head, tried to get back on his feet pushing on the seat with both his hands. I helped the lady to get on her feet, braced her shoulder to support and escorted them to the nearby Ancient Travellers Inn.

The receptionist handed me the key to Room number 9, with a creaky floor, worn out circular staircase, eerie bedroom with twin beds. By the time we got to their bedroom I noticed they had no strength in their legs, Elsie just managed to crawl to her bed panting for breath and flopped exhausted. Aldhelm told his wife, "Elsie it had been a long hard day for you waiting to see Emily and Arthur. You are tired, lie down and rest, would you like to eat something now?" She did not reply. Aldhelm continued, "You did not even eat your egg and cress sandwich at lunch time".

I was touched by the soft caring voice of Aldhelm, as if he was talking to his little sister who was unwell !! Elsie did not respond, she dozed off, fell asleep like a tired child.

Aldhelm came to see me off to the reception. We sat down in the empty lounge, I ordered two beer. He told me that they have been coming to Wells cathedral for many many years, usually at Easter time. He added, "Elsie likes to visit the cathedral at this time of the year when Emily and Arthur visit the town ... I am not Elsie's husband; I was a Luftwaffe pilot in charge of one the Messerschmidt Bf 109. I was shot down by a Spitfire on 7 September 1940 in the Battle of Britain. It was John who was guiding the gun aiming at me at the cockpit from his Spitfire. We were so close, we could see each other eyes.

Aldhelm paused for a short time and said, "Something happened, John did not fire at me, instead turned his 20mm cannon at the fuselage of my plane under the cockpit. I jumped out and landed on the ground safely in my parachute. I saw my plane coming down like a ball of fire whirling round and round like a ball of fire.

I asked him, "Why do you think John changed his mind?".

Aldhelm said "I don't know for sure but I think John was frightened as a new pilot. We were taught that success in this game comes once you subdue fear. Once you shot down two or three planes, the effect is terrific and you carry on shooting until you kill your target or get yourself killed.

He might have thought war is part of a game and he forgot the risks. He was killed the next day."

I asked Aldhelm, "Do you sometimes see flashback of that day?"

Aldhelm nodded, "Yes many many times. I remember how the Squadron leader sent for me the night before and said, "Young man, tomorrow is the day you will fight on your own. He said we have lost many of our experienced pilots in last two weeks, I am confident you will know what to do for the best".

That night, suddenly it dawned on me that I will be all alone on that plane flying over the enemy's domain. If I make a single mistake, mishandle instruments or commit an error, that will be the end of me and my plane. I was not confident enough to rely upon my own skill, there will be no one to relieve me if I fault. I found out we lost eight out of our sixteen aircrafts which were shot down in last two weeks. Two of them at close range of sixty feet. They told me that if I feel lonely, I should talk to other pilots on the radio for company and support. Many of our pilots died of burnt out and did not survive.

They put me at the POW camp here in Wells at Stoberry park. After the war many German prisoners were sent to harsh labour camps in Europe. I was released in 1946. We were treated well here in Britain. We used to work on the fields helping farmers bringing in the harvest. Many of the politicians of that time were sympathetic towards POWs. British public also demanded that government treat us well and repatriate us as soon as possible. I was a Berlin boy; I did not want to return to Berlin as it was under Soviet rule. I was also attending a course on re-orientation in democratic politics.

I decided to settle in London as many of my compatriots were there. After a while I decided to find out the pilot who shot my plane down. After some enquires, I found out who the pilot was, it was John Smith, of No.19 Squadron RAF Luton, 26 years old. John was shot down the following day, 8 September 1940, when he died. I wanted to meet his family, tell them about John's kindness. When I found Elsie, I told them how John saved my life. Elsie listened to me very quietly, then said, "John's dad was a man of cloth, he told John not to harm anyone if he can, we are all children of God. He then told John the story of Mary Ellis the RAF pilot whose life was saved by a Luftwaffe pilot in the Battle of Britain."

There was a black and white wedding photograph of John and Elsie on the mental piece of their sitting room. I looked at the picture, they looked so young, John in his RAF uniform without his helmet and Elsie in her wedding outfit. I saw the wedding cake and Elsie smiling like a blushing happy new bride. I said to Elsie "you had a lovely cake for your wedding". Elsie said, "No that was a cardboard cover decorated with plaster and painted white to look like a luxury wedding cake".

Elsie said, "We only invited our parents as we had to make do and mend as there was rationing and shortages all over the country. I told Elsie it was same in Germany. I was touched by Elsie's honesty. I did not return to Germany and settled down in London".

I met Elsie again when she phoned me one day to tell that Emily and Arthur, her grandson died in an accident on the motorway to Wells to see the Cathedral on a stormy day. It was the Easter time 1965.

I came to see Elsie: I told her, "Your husband saved my life; I shall be there for you any time if I can help."

We have been keeping in touch with each other since that time. As you can see Elsie's mind gets confused, her memory is poor, she hallucinates of her family more often than before. Her only wish in life is to see her family at Wells Cathedral every Easter time. I told her we are getting old; maybe this is the last time we shall visit Wells Cathedral and no more". Aldhelm sat back on his chair, he took a long breath to recover.

I did a bit of research about paranormal sightings of a young child and his mum near the Chapter house steps. Yes, there was recorded appearance of such a couple in 1954 and again in 2005. I wonder if Elsie was right all along, or was it her hallucination?

Next morning, I went to the hotel to take them to the Bus station. The hotel door was open, I saw James the receptionist and asked if Elsie and Aldhelm had their breakfast to take them to the Bus station. James said they are still in their room; he was waiting for them to come down. I went up, Aldhelm said Elsie was still in the bath room, she seemed to be very confused last night. After waiting for some time Aldhelm knocked the bath room door, no one answered, he pushed the door, Elsie was not there. I followed him down to the reception, James confirmed that when he came in that morning the main door was open, he had not seen anyone there.

We went out looking for Elsie, she was sitting on the same bench in front of the Chapter house steps. Elsie did not recognise me or Aldhelm at all. She was confused, raised her hand and felt her forehead as if to indicate that she had a headache, Aldhelm touched her head and said, "You got a swelling here, how did it happen; did you fall down?" Elsie did not reply.

Elsie did not recognise either of us, she kept saying "where am I? what am I doing here?" After a while she asked again, "How did I get here? What day is today?" I checked her legs and arms, I suspected she might have had a stroke. I told Aldhelm I am sending for an emergency ambulance for her to go to hospital. When the ambulance arrived, they told us her blood pressure was sky high, she needed to go to hospital. We were barred from going with her due to suspected Covid-19 infection. Aldhelm was very worried and sad for not being allowed to visit her in hospital. He was lost for word and nodded. Elsie was hospitalised for next seven days while Aldhelm stayed in the hotel.

I visited Aldhelm most evenings to update about Elsie's progress after phoning the ward and also tried to give him company as best as I could. The sister from hospital told me on phone, "we have completed all investigations and got the brain scan report. Her blood pressures have come down since she started taking her medications, we noticed she was under a lot of stress which some time can cause similar symptoms, may be due to loneliness and Covid-19 isolation".

Luckily the hotel management agreed to help the old couple considering their long-time association. Young James at the reception who we found very helpful, took care of the breakfast, and arranged for take away dinner.

One day I asked Aldhelm if he still keeps in touch with family in Germany. He looked sad and said he had not had any contact with his family for a long time and unaware of their address. The last time he met one of his nephews was many years ago when he came to London School of Economics to study and lost contact after he returned home to Germany. I asked him, "Do you still think of home some time?" Aldhelm said, "Yes now that I have lots of time on my hands, I wonder, life could have been so much better in a world without the war". I asked again, "Would you like to go back to Berlin for a visit?".

Aldhelm said, "Maybe now, that all those Russians are gone". "Do you remember the name of your nephew?"

After a pause he said, "Yes, his name was Luke, Luke Gruber. He sent me a card from Munich many years ago after he returned home finishing his degree at the London School of Economics".

"What about your sister?", I asked.

Aldhelm said, "I have forgotten the faces of all my brothers, but I still remember my only sister". We were a big family, six boys and a girl, she was the youngest, we used to be very close as all my brothers joined the Army and were sent away to the Eastern front.

Later I joined the Luftwaffe. All five brothers were sent to Stalingrad, and my sister was sent to Linz in Austria to be safe with one of our distant relative, an aunt. All my brothers died; I am the one who survived.

I do not exactly know what happened to my sister, I came to know that my sister first got involved with an American G.I. and got pregnant when she was about 19 years old. She had many boyfriends and when the baby was born, she did not know who his father was. My aunt later told Luke, "After your mum had the baby, she stayed with me for a short time. One day she suddenly disappeared leaving the baby in his cot with note saying, "Soon I shall return and take the baby home once I've settled down". Luke told me my sister never returned to take him back home. Our aunt had no children and she brought up Luke on her own.

"I never had any contact with my sister, but I met Luke when he came to do his studies in London school of Economics in 1966."

I could not believe my ears, Luke Gruber, could he be my old friend Luke who has just retired as the boss of that big international bank?, I wondered. May be Luke Gruber is a common name in Germany. I did not ask as Aldhelm was very tired that night worrying about Elsie.

Three days later Elsie was discharged from hospital. When I came to collect them to the Bus station Aldhelm handed a hospital report to me and said, "They said Elsie did not have a stroke, she had an episode of transient global amnesia, what is it?". I "Googled" it and explained, "that's to do with severe mental stress, she will recover soon", I picked them up and took them to the Bus station.

I explained to the driver their situation and asked him to keep an eye on the old couple. I also told him that they will get off the bus at Golders Green Station as they live close by. I gave Aldhelm my card and said, "please let me know if I can be of any help in the future".

Yesterday I went for my routine walk, looked at the bench where Elsie and Aldhelm used to sit, there was no one for me to see except for the memory of a brief encounter with a couple of strangers sharing a moment of history.

George Harrison and his ukulele

❖ ❖ ❖

"There's was a time that I remember, when I did not know pain, I believed in forever, and everything would stay the same".

So sang the Beatles in 1967. As I went through life, I know every age is a passing phase. I remember George Harrison's song:

"I don't want you
But I hate to lose you
you got me in-between
The Devil and the deep blue sea!"

Those words made me sad, "it was cruel", I thought, to cause George so much of hurt. I reminisced those words, and I still can feel the hurt he had to endure.

I read about George's friendship with Sitar maestro Ravi Shankar. Shankar wrote in his autobiography that once when he was flying in an aeroplane, suddenly he thought of compiling a song in English and wrote it down when he got back home. This was the first song he wrote in English.

"I am missing you Krishna*
Where are you?
Though I can't see you
I hear your flute

---
* Krishna in Hinduism was reincarnation of God.

Please come wipe my tears
And make me smile
Where are you Krishna?
Where are you?"

The song was probably a yearning, a sense of loneliness, missing his home, being cut off from friends, family and culture, living away in a foreign country far from his God.

Ravi Shankar told his friend and pupil George Harrison about the song he wrote.

George was a deeply spiritual man, a catholic by birth. At that time George was experimenting with drugs and LSD, western music, eastern spirituality, Rock, women and his long-held faith.

When George heard Shankar's sitar recital, he might have noticed the similarity of the dainty, nimble sound of his much-loved ukulele.

After reading Shankar's song George told Shankar that he liked his song, so much that he wanted to do a version of the song of his own.

George's song:

"I Don't want you,
But I hate to lose you
You got me in-between
The devil and the deep blue sea,
Fate seems to give my heart a twist
And I keep running back for more"

(by Devil, did he mean his addictions?)

Was it a cry for help deep down from his tormented soul? Or was it someone who declined his young ardent love? Critics agree that most of the time, George Harrison let his music do the talking.

On his final assessment of life George said –

"... the time will come when you see we are all one and life flow on with you and without you, the ego is the eternal problem, all things must pass".

I am a hero[*]

❖ ❖ ❖

I used to be a wimp
I was scared to rock the boat
in case I get into trouble
I sat quietly, agreed politely in case you crush me to rubble
You held me down, pushed me to the mirror
I saw my own eyes blazing like fire
Like a wounded tiger raving in anger
I roared like a lion
I jumped out and kicked your belly
Fast as Muhammad Ali
Dancing through the fight, floating like a butterfly
Stinging like a bee
I etched my name in the in the book of history
I earned my stripes
I am a champion
I went from zero to my own hero
I am a champion
I am a hero.

---

[*] This poem was inspired by Katy Perry's poem "ROAR"

Happy days

❖ ❖ ❖

We were singing "Bohemian Rhapsody", and made up our words

> "Easy come, easy go, will you not let him go. (Let him go!)
> Bismillah! We will not let you go. (Let him go!)

He went on repeating:

> Just get out, just gotta get right outa here
> (oooh, ooh, yeah, ooh, yeah ...)"

Mum was cooking, heard us (me and my friend Rudy, rocking like two mad man) jumping

> On my bed making a racket of everything around.

Then Rudy decided to change the singing:

> "I want to be free
> We are the champions
> Friends will be friends"

Pitch went up and up. Mum could not put up with all that nonsense.
   She came in, when she saw the damage, she sent for Rudy's mum.

They inspected the damage, books on the floor, bedsheet torn apart, squirted paint on my new carpet. It was a total disaster.

Rudy's mum was very angry, we were ordered to keep away from our X-Boxes and restricted from meeting each other for a week.

On the third day sitting in my room, I saw the photograph of two us playing happily in the snow. It made me happy and I smiled.

Looking back, I thought to myself friendship is a luxury being together with my friends.

As I grew up, I thought I had many friends with golden heart.

Be happy, memories are for ever.

Reminiscing my college days

❖ ❖ ❖

Introduction

It all started with an email from my old friend Dr Kokil Barua. I was walking along my usual route for my routine exercise. I heard my mobile ping, I stopped and sat on a bench next to the beautiful moat and looked at my mobile message. The message said, "Utpal we are planning a virtual get together with all our friends next Saturday at 6.30 pm IST. You are invited join us on that day."

Like a flash, my memories went back to our younger years when we, a group of strangers bonded together like a big family, nurtured by our Alma Mater Assam Medical College.

As I made my way to the College, I saw the long green avenue, clean rain-washed tea gardens and an immaculate two-way drive, never seen a place like that anywhere before in Assam. I think that was the moment when I fell in love with that place, smitten till this day.

Soon I got to know most of my classmates. My life changed in a different trajectory, that of a future doctor. Over the years we came to know each other and learned to respect and avoid people given one the freedom to choose close friends.

Before we moved to the premises of Assam Medical College, we spent our Pre-medical year at Berry White Medical School nearer to Dibrugarh town.

Among the group of new friends, I met Samarkant Singh (Soram) and his best mate was Jodha Singh (Sanasam) from Manipur with impeccable academic achievements.

Since our reunion, we caught up with each other and talked about the events of our lives during the intervening years.

Today I received an email from one of my friends that contained a sweet surprise, it said "Utpal there is plan to publish a book on Dr Jodha Sanasam. Will you please write a brief biographical note about his time at Assam Medical College?".

That did put my thoughts in a spin, tangled memories of fifty years in the past gradually unravelled in my mind.

Here is how I can remember my time at Assam Medical College (AMC).

The year was 1962. We were the first batch to join the Medical College as pre-medical students when Intermediate course was abolished in Assam. Our admission was marred by confusion due to change of curriculum, more importantly at that time China invaded Assam causing added distractions. While Chinese invaded Assam, suddenly the government of the day realised that India was poorly equipped to stop such unforeseen situation. The Army was ill equipped to defend the country, unprepared to face the enemy, scores of injured Jawans suffered from lack of medical treatment due to lack of trained doctors. Finally, the Indian government decided to increase the number of seats at Assam Medical College by 50 seats in pre-medical course. Looking back, now I feel, for people like me, this change of plan of the Government of the day turned out to be a blessing in disguise. I joined other fellow students at the Berry White Medical School dormitory. I was surprised to find that the additional group of entrants included Samar Kanta Singh and Jodha Singh two other beneficiary of extended list of students. They both did brilliantly in their academic career, yet they were not eligible to join as medical student at Assam Medical College due to bureaucratic nightmares of that time. Only because of their perseverance and determination both managed to get enrolled in Assam Medical College when additional seats were allocated to them. Here is a report from one of the most distinguished doctors of Manipur, Lamabam Kamal Sing wrote about the plight of both Jodha and Samar while they applied for Medical College admission:

> "Jodha was selected for Pre-medical Course at Bankura Medical College, West Bengal. When he reported there, he was informed that the college would not be able to arrange extra teachers for English alternative, and thus Bengali Vernacular was compulsory and mandatory. Jodha happened to apply to Assam Medical College (AMC). Samar Kanta, the brilliant boy who, from St Edmund's

college, Shillong was placed at the second position at Pre-university Course under Guahati University was also denied admission, as Samar had no sponsorship from the government (of Manipur); Jodha fought back hard in the office of the Health and Medical Secretariat".

Finally, both of them were admitted to AMC after a long struggle with bureaucratic hurdles and both arrived at our Pre-Medical course two months later. I recently came to know from Samar, to be at AMC was the fulfilment of his family aspirations. He told me recently that his father was a student at the Berry White Medical School, unfortunately constraints of personal nature made it impossible for him to continue his studies.

Soon our Pre-Medical year came to an end. We now moved to the premises of Assam Medical college. For me and my friends that was the time when our lives changed for ever.

Pre-Clinical Years
In the first two years at Medical college, we learned Anatomy, Biochemistry, Physiology and organic Chemistry.

The Anatomy Dissection Hall was a long rectangular room. Fifty dissection tables made of white marble where specimen (dead bodies) were laid in lines for us to work upon. All those bodies were dark black in colour. One would get the smell of formalin (that made me feel nauseous for a long time to come) that clung to our clothes. We arrived at 8 am every morning in our white coats to learn every bits of a human body at a time.

Clinical Years
Once we finished with our Pre-clinical studies, we moved to our third-year studies. Most exciting event was that from now

on we could hang a stethoscope around our neck just to show off that we were now budding doctors. The subjects we studied were Pathology, Pharmacology Social and Preventive medicine and Forensic medicine. Plus, all the mandatory clinical subjects.

As we approached our last and final year, we had to work harder, make decisions and take responsibilities, for self, for our future patients, and our families.

That was the time when we changed from being care-free adolescents to more serious individuals. Exposure to real patient-care exposes one to realities of a doctor's life. Most of us devoted longer hours to our studies, average between 3 hours to 6 hours a day.

I remember Jodha was a naturally gifted person with a sharp intelligence, he always tried to help others when one approached him for his help.

He was well versed in music, easy going, open minded and interested in local culture. At that time none of us knew that he had hidden talents in Literature, Photography and Philosophical discourse. He was seen singing and playing musical instruments at times and very social in nature.

Around that time something else happened to his life. He appeared to be more cheerful and happy. We did not know what made him so happy (may be Samar was the only person who knew his secret).

Later I came to know, he found a beautiful girl and he fell head over heels in love with her. In due course they got married to each other. Time moved on; their love blossomed with a beautiful family like a fairy tale story.

After our finals we started our Pre-registration rotating housemen ship programme with lots of excitement and enthusiasm. That was the crowning period of two years Pre-medical, four years medical school training plus another year of Rotational houseman ship. Suddenly it dawned on us that the safety and security of supervised patient care will not be available once we leave AMC. The responsibilities of making decisions on life and death matters of our patients would depend entirely on one's shoulders. A daunting prospect for a newly qualified doctor.

By Winter of 1968, we said goodbye to our friends and to our beloved Alma mater, Assam Medical College with heavy hearts and misty eyes.

Looking back to my fifty years as a Doctor, I believe the most important ingredient of a good doctor has not changed, "Medical profession is a feat, it requires self-sacrifice, purity of soul and purity of thoughts" (Anton Povolovich Chekov).

All I want to say to you my friend Jodha, you are a very special person, you deserve the best, you are a man of many wishes, you did it all your own and you are famously successful.

Best wishes always.

Revisit to The Grange

❖ ❖ ❖

I got back to England after nearly twenty years in February 2020 for a business meeting in London.

I had to extend my stay for the "C" virus and decided to pay a visit to my old home in Bristol. I was born in that house and still think of it as my home. Since Dad died my only contact with Bristol was the phone number of old nanny Mrs Beatrice. I was imagining nanny Betty in her beige uniform. Mum wanted everyone to know their station in life, she was status conscious, liked to show off her diamonds; now she deals with fine jewellery for millionaires in Paris.

I felt a mixture of emotions as the city changed beyond recognition. Next morning, I took a cab to my old address, not knowing what to expect in my old house. When I arrived, I could not see the house I knew so well. There was a new house built with reclaimed stone with a "For sale" sign. It had a large manicured garden and woodland. I approached the main gate and saw a gentleman talking to his gardener. They looked at me and the gentleman asked who I was looking for. I asked him if he knew nanny Beatrice who used to live in the annex of the old house.

The man smiled and said, "Oh, nanny Beatrice, yes she lives in that ground floor flat in the annex, she is still there, I shall come with you, if that's okay with you".

He introduced himself as the owner of the place. The garden looked lovely on that glorious spring morning with magnificent bursts of colour all around.

Nanny Beatrice did not recognise me until I spoke, and my unexpected arrival threw her into some confusion; it was not until I had been sitting some time by her fireside that she recovered her old calm. She had changed so little in her manners all these years since I knew her, although she had become greatly aged.

Once she recognised me I was Denise, her eyes filled with tears, she was so pleased to see me ..., ... so was I. Richard, the owner was still there watching two of us in bewilderment when Beatrice told him that I was the daughter of Henry the Seventh, who owned the original property since 1695.

I noted a burst of excitement on Richard's face. He asked me if I can spare some time to talk to him about something which may be of mutual interest. He works at the City Museum. I agreed to have a chat with him once I finish with Beatrice.

We finished cups of tea and chatted about old times. Beatrice said, "I have been thinking of you a lot lately. Your dad, before he passed away asked me to give you this small package. I thought I shall never see you again."

I took the package and gave Beatrice a hug, kissed her and said good bye.

I met Richard afterwards. He said, "your ancestors hid some stuff in the basement of your old house. I have been trying to find your family for years. Did you know Henry the First was one of the most prolific pirates in maritime history of the last five hundred years?"

"No, not really, all I know was that he was like a Robin Hood of the Seas, robbed the rich and paid the poor", I replied.

Richard said, "When the original house was pulled down, we found lots of stuff in the basement. The strong room was empty, there were lots of nautical artefacts still left behind".

I told him that as none of the family now lived in England, he could give away whatever he found in the basement to the local museum.

Richard said, "Once your seafaring ancestor pulled off his most spectacular heist on 7 September 1695. He and his men captured the Ganj-i-Sawai, a vessel of Emperor Aurangzeb of India; full of rubies, ivory, gold and silver bullion worth about £16 billion of today's money".

"Emperor Aurangzeb?" I asked.

Richard replied, "He was the son of Emperor Shah Jahan who built the Taj mahal."

I looked at my old house. When I saw the tarnished brass plate; "The Grange" at the gate, I cried again.

I opened my gift; it was an unusual small piece of exotic pink diamond.

This story was inspired by: "A true story of Piracy, Power and History of First Global Manhunt" by Steven Johnson.

The aftermath

❖ ❖ ❖

It fell upon me to break the news. They said "Rana, we think you are the right person to approach the family, Ajay was a good friend of yours, you know his wife well and kids think of you as one of the family".

I said, "Give me some time, I know I did this many time before, but this is different, Ajay was not only my colleague, he was my best friend. It is different today to meet his family and tell the bad news. I got to get my narrative right; I am flummoxed myself".

I tried to work out what I will be telling them and how shall I say it? How will I tell them Ajay has passed away? I have to calm down, manage my thoughts, rein in my own emotions, running high, out of control. I must do this because he was my best friend. I have to leave now, before the bad news reaches his family. There are pressmen sniffing for bad news all over the place.

I hurried to Ajay's flat, knocked the door, tried to look calm and composed. His daughter Rita opened the door. I did not know she has returned home that night from her university. She smiled and said, "Mum it's uncle Rana coming to see you". Sita was in the kitchen, I got the aroma of freshly cooked Biryani wafting from the kitchen, she smiled at me and asked me in.

"I did not expect you at this time, anyway come in, you are always welcome".

Suddenly all my prepared narrative disappeared in the thin air, I huddled both mum and daughter and said, "Ajay has passed away". The room was filled with an air of total disbelief. Sita said, "Tell me Rana, what happened?". I explained, "We don't know yet his cause of death, he was working in the ITU, he looked very exhausted, then he passed out. The nurse said that he was in the ward for the last three days without a break. He looked ill. He did not complain of any chest pain. We found him holding a GTN (Glyceryl Trinitrate) spray in his hand, he collapsed and passed away."

Sita put her hand on my shoulder, "Ajay thought of you like his own brother", she asked me, "Were you there with him when his life ended?".

Sita did not cry, as if she was expecting the bad news since Covid-19 arrived in England.

The Prime minister proclaimed Thursdays as the celebration day for the NHS heroes who gave their time and lives for the NHS and the victims of an unprecedented pandemic disaster.

Every week down the street, at 8 pm on Thursdays people opened their doors and windows to applaud, the Church bells rang to remind citizens to pay their respects to NHS workers for their selfless struggles and strife to save life against a virulent virus.

They will never know how it feels to lose one's loved one in such an avalanche of death never seen before.

Rita, stood in the darkness behind her house, said to herself, "I don't want to worship my Dad as a hero, it causes such heart wrenching pain to think that he will never come home again ... please stop, we too are dying inside us while we are still alive".

The brave new world

❖ ❖ ❖

September 2050

I was ready for a trip to hospital. I was invited to go for my centenary check-up.

At 08:00 hours my eyes flicked with 6 dots indicating that I have an appointment at Work station 32, at our local Health service station. The message from the Booking Booth arrived with a list of instructions,

"Dear Patient, we have noticed that you are now six weeks overdue for your annual check-up. According to our electronic data assessment, it appears that you need a full check-up as recommended by your Healthcare Manual.

If you are unable to visit physically due to impaired locomotion or any other associated dysfunction, we can offer you alternative transport including direct vaporisation and reconstitution facilities.

As per General Medical Council regulations, we are obliged to inform you that there is 0.9% chance of failure of such transportation methodology. According to Government Regulation HS 798 Section 876b, we the provider of services are exempt from paying any compensation in case we are unable to reconstitute you to your original form as the system is currently undergoing clinical trial. You might have seen such reports of 'failure to revert patients' to original state in the National Tribune, which is correct as per today's report.

For further details please consult 'Reconstitution PDF 0090765 dated 30.9.24'.

Looking forward to meet you soon as per schedule."

I decided to visit for my check up on my 10-year-old electronic air mobile. I do have a bit of reduced mobility since my knees were replaced 5 years ago. I was told because of my exercise routine of running 10 miles marathon on a daily basis, the platinum caps of both knees have worn off. However they will review my knees and replace them as indicated in the future. They are a bit concerned about my heart beats which was reported irregular at times, but due to financial austerity in the NHS and lack of healthy dead heart, I am currently on the waiting list for heart transplant.

After I had my tests (by the AI robot Heart specialist), I was informed that it will discuss my results with its colleague in Kidney and Lung specialist for future management in due course. I shall be closely monitored by mobile apps, no need for attending a doctor's office or a hospital.

I was also informed that the current set up is rather antiquated and will cease to exist in the near future. The new proposed system will facilitate convergence of technology, digitalization and 3D modelling. The advent of nanotechnology will usher in age of Nanomedicine which will diagnose, treat and prevent various diseases.

The government recently approved £32m of funds to provide us with immortality. Hence some scientists started a clinical trial to check how to keep the population under control by releasing Covid-24. Watch out soon there will be another similar trial of Anthrax like illness all over the world.

The future

❖ ❖ ❖

I looked in the mirror this morning, I saw an old man with white hair.
His face has not changed the slightest since I saw him last time.
I have seen that face thousands of times before.
I could not work out when that changed from a boy to a man then to a curmudgeon.
Surreptitiously recording age without my recognition.
This morning I got the news that my uncle passed away.
Another victim of the onslaught of Covid-19 affliction.
I looked through the window and saw the blooming roses.
A beautiful garden, that survived storm, torrential rain and scorching summer sun.
One day when I look back to the summer of 2020, will it be loaded with.
Sadness in my heart or the memory of those sweet-smelling roses?
I shall remember my friends from the Wells writing group.
For their support and warmth that keep renewing my dwindling hopes.
Time will wash away the sadness of this year.
We shall move on with confidence without fear.

The goddess of Cu Chi tunnels

❖ ❖ ❖

Last summer we visited Vietnam for a short holiday. We were a group of fifteen retired people, some from England, some from New Zealand and Australia. I met an Australian called Rodney on our trip to Cu Chi tunnels near Ho Chi Min City. When we arrived, first impression was that of an impoverished theme park of woods and tunnels. The place had a sad history, where thousands died, mutilated and emotionally scarred during their struggle for independence.

It all started in 1940s when Vietnamese fought for freedom from their erstwhile French masters. They dug miles of tunnels for guerrilla warfare, finally, defeated the French at the Dien Bien Phu battle. Soon the American marched in to stop the Communists from taking over Indo-China. Brutal war continued with indiscriminate all-round attacks, bombardments to eliminate Vietnamese communists, civilians and peasants.

Final death toll was 1.1 million Vietnamese, 250 000 South Vietnamese soldiers, 80 000 US servicemen, still counting the missing numbers.

By the time we arrived at the Cu Chi Tunnels. I noticed Rodney appeared to be a bit at unease with the place, I thought he was worrying about the prospect of walking through those narrow slippery muddy tunnels with his limp right leg.

I asked him if he was alright. He said he had been there a number of times when he was an Australian volunteer as part of coalition with US Army in 1960s Vietnam war.

Rodney said, "I shall tell you my bit of a story later tonight".

That evening I heard Rodney's Story.

Rodney told me, "These tunnels were narrow, 16m diameter, 3m deep, 50cm wide, and 80cm high, spread over 250 km where people lived, dined, met and fought. There were places of worship, hospital, children were born, had places for relaxation, it was an underground parallel world".

Rodney was a keen caver, he joined the American tunnel Rats, the unit to search and demolish those tunnels. He said, "One day three of us were assigned to destroy a tunnel. Each carried a C3 gun, a torch and a pack of lunch and hand grenades. After crawling for an hour, we ended up in a very strange place. The leader carefully approached the entrance to a secret chamber. There was a group of standing people behind a tarpaulin cover in front of a statue of a woman. Her torso was that of a human upper half, legs were like that of a crouching octopus. She was protected by a group of people with ice cold eyes in complete silence. They were all dead human guarding a goddess. Suddenly there was a crunching noise, I saw a door closing behind me, I shouted 'get out, get out'; I crawled out as fast as I could. That's when I trapped my right leg. I was lucky to be alive."

I asked Rodney, "What happened to your mates in that dead-end chamber?"

"I lead the second search team looking for those fallen soldiers. We found the Goddess and the standing dead. I shined my light, saw two piles of ashes in human shape next to their guns. I took photos and returned to base. When I reported to the C.O., he took out a pair of magnifying glass, he said, "Photos looked like bodies burnt by napalm bombs.

He sent for the specialists, they suspected they were victims of spontaneous self-combustion. The Padre was appalled, "They defiled a sacred place, an act so profane and wicked, they paid the price".

Someone sent for the village shaman, his opinion, "It was an evil act of sorcery no doubt". Then the Shaman submitted a bill to C.O. Mahony. C.O. looked at the bill, exclaimed, "Five dollars? I am not sure H.Q. in Saigon will approve such a high amount for ten minutes consultation."

The Shaman was not pleased with such a response. He said, "the Government here is total rubbish; they charge 50% tax plus Vat if you earn above fifteen dollars a month. You can give me three dollars fifty cents' cash, if it's alright".

C.O. Mahony fished out his wallet from his pocket, gave a five-dollar bill and said to Shaman, "Keep the change for your travel expenses".

As soon as the old man left, we all laughed out loud, gloom disappeared.

"Colonel Mahony was a fine man; he knew the names of all men under his command". Rodney reminisced and sighed.

Rodney was tired, I asked him to retire.

Next day I went out on another excursion. On my return I had a shower and went to the bar for a drink hoping to meet Rodney there. The waiter who served us drinks the night before asked me if I heard the news, he then told me Rodney committed suicide last night in the hotel swimming pool. I was shocked, I told him, "Well that wasn't what I'd expected at all!".

I wondered, was he a victim of a curse or was it post-combat mental disorder?

The unsung hero

❖ ❖ ❖

Part One

On a hot summer day in 2013, we arrived at Gallipoli, located in the southern part of East Thrace in Turkey, close to the Aegean Sea to the west and the Dardanelles straight to the east. We were a group of ten people from UK and except for me and my wife, the rest of the party were keen to visit the huge Commonwealth war cemetery close to the hills.

The Turkish Guide told us briefly about the history of that place with a sense of pride. He told us about the great disasters of WWI when between 25 April 1915 and 9 January 1916 the Ottoman Empire defeated the Allied troops including British, Anzacs and Indian Army corps. The Ottoman troops under Field Marshal Ataturk after the defeat of Allied troops became the founding father of the Republic of Turkey.

After the introduction we were directed to the graveyard where there were rows of graves with names and DoB/DoD engraved on them. I saw at least four graves of Anzac soldiers who were under the age of fifteen in that graveyard. When I asked the guide how those kids were enlisted in the Army so young, he said those boys probably lied about their age as girls used to call them cowards if they did not volunteer to join the Army. Sometimes to embarrass young boys, girls presented them with feathers to put the boys to shame.

Suddenly I remembered, a friend of mine once told me that his grandfather was an Indian Sepoy who volunteered to fight for the British in WWI. He was one of the young men who died in the Gallipoli campaign. His family inherited a medal for his bravery and later he became a legend in his village for the sacrifices he made for the sake of duty. Up to 15,000 Indians fought in Gallipoli, they belonged to the 29th Indian Infantry Brigade and "the Mule Corps of unsung heroes of Gallipoli".

As I could not find any tomb of an Indian soldier in that graveyard, I asked the guide where did they cremate the dead Indians? He said in Haydarpasa Cemetery, near Istanbul.

Churchill spear-headed the military debacle in Gallipoli, 250 000 casualties including 46 000 deaths, a costly failure, now a forgotten history.

Part Two
Last Christmas my brother phoned me to tell me that one of my Nepali friends visited him.

Recently in India. His name was Dr Vijoy Thapa, after a pause I remembered my old friend. My brother said Dr Thapa wanted to talk to me as he will be visiting London soon to attend a conference. He asked for my phone number as he did not know anyone else in London. I was pleased to hear about Vijoy after all those years and asked my brother if Vijoy gave his phone number for me to contact directly. After I got Vijoy's number I phoned him, we tried to catch up about our lives and chatted for ages.

Vijoy was a clever student, he joined our college on a scholarship and did well professionally over the years. I remember once he told me that his great-grandfather was in the British Army who died in action in the Western front many years ago. After he died his family received war compensation and with that money his family provided a good education to Vijoy.

Vijoy arrived in London on a cold February morning from New Delhi this year. I picked him up from Terminal 3 and brought him home for a few days.

After a good natter, he asked me, "Can I ask you for a favour?". He then told me that before his grandma passed away about a year ago, one day she showed Vijoy part of a letter from the War Office in London. Vijoy showed me a note, a brown old document to read,

Re: Burial Location of Corporal Bhim Bahadur Thapa.

"The number of plots is indicated by a Roman numeral following the entry, the row by a capital letter, and the grave number.

Thus II.B.34 indicates plot II, row B and grave number 34.

Corporal Thapa was interred at the above plot in Chattri crematorium in Brighton. England."

Vijoy said, "Grandma's last wish, was to ask me to visit her father's funeral site. She always thought about her dad with great sadness as he died without his family in a faraway corner of the Earth, the family felt granddad's soul would always be in a limbo as his funeral was incomplete without a proper Hindu religious ceremony."

I could see Vijoy's eyes a bit misty with emotions thinking about his granny. I told him as he will be staying with us for a few days I shall take him to Brighton and see the hospital where his granddad was a patient after his injury in the western front. On the way I told him about how the original spectacular Royal Pavilions in Brighton was converted to a Dome Hospital for injured Indian army with 680 beds in seaside palaces and fitted with all available modern conveniences. As we approached

Brighton, I pointed out the beautiful Brighton pavilion. Vijoy appeared to be lost in his thoughts and did not much take in whatever I was talking about.

We arrived at Chattri war memorial in late afternoon. It was a nice cool day with soft winter sunshine. Although neither of us knew that morning, we were told that the crematorium was completed only a few days ago on 1 February 2020. The foundation stone was laid in August 1920. The place had a feel of pilgrimage, a marble War memorial reflecting its architectural and historic importance. I noted Vijoy's demeanour changed as we walked up the 500 feet elevation looking southwards toward Brighton. We were told bodies of 63 Hindus and Sikhs were taken to a remote location, cremated and their ashes were scattered in the English Channel.

I walked away towards the seaside, leaving Vijoy to absorb the enormous weight of history spanning three generations of his family.

The Chattri Memorial Brighton. United Kingdom

Vijoy took off his shoes at the bottom of the steps, bowed his head to say a little prayer, as if he would have done back at home in a temple.

After paying his homage, Vijoy walked down the steps in a poignant mood, he bent down and picked a bit of dirt and a small pebble. With folded hands he kneeled down and uttered a prayer to his ancestors. Then he saw me and said, "I shall put these in our family shrine at home, granddad will never be alone anymore."

On our way back home in silence, I played a Hindi song: Zindegi Ki Safar*

Here is an English version of the song for you to muse upon:

"Life is a wonderful journey
No one knows what will happen in the future
We have to go ahead to the Moon and the Stars
We have to reach beyond the skies
The world will be left behind
Who knows what's in the future?
... No one knows what the future holds.
... here at rest are so many unknown people
Life is a lonely journey ..."

As we approached home, Vijoy hugged me gently and said, "Thanks, my friend, I had been dreaming of this day for a very long time".

---

* The song was written by Hasrat Jaipuri. Music by Sankar Jaikishan. Singer Kishore Kumar.

A quick visit to Manhattan, New York

❖ ❖ ❖

It was a bright summer morning, I was waiting for a mail,
My heart jumped with a bag of expectations ... the letter has arrived.
It said "You can join us as soon as you are ready"
I had a premonition that the letter would bring some magical news;
So, I decided to share the good news,
Told my family, "We are on our way to New York City, the city that never sleeps".
The words of Frank Sinatra kept ringing in my ears

> "I am leaving today; I want to be part of it
> New York, New York.
> I am goanna make a brand-new start of it
> In old New York"

In my mind I made a plan to visit the Statue of Liberty, the Empire State Building, the Metropolitan Museum of Art, Time Square, Broadway & Macy's Departmental store & more. Our first priority was to the Empire State Building, we went up to the 86th floor, where you can enjoy a view of the city.

Next stop was the Statue of Liberty, built by Gustav Eiffel, I could not climb the 146 steps of the spiral staircase.

Then we proceeded to the world-famous Metropolitan Museum of Art (MET). We saw the painting, "The Death of

Socrates", who was convicted of corrupting Athenian Society and was sentenced to death by poison (hemlock) for his crime.

We saw the dancing beautiful celestial deity from India (Devata) sculpted by ancient Hindu artists of a long-gone time.

We hurried through the first floor, glancing at the Sphinx of Hatshepsut on way out of the building.

We went for a cold drink and an ice-cream in a busy café by the side of the Park Avenue. A young lady came to serve us, she was moaning about a rude customer. She told us, "That man thinks I am just another waitress, what he does not know is that my other job is a real estate owner, I only do this job because Wall Street is not doing well these days".

As the sun got hotter, we made our way to Times Square where we saw a Naked Cowboy

Singing rude songs and strumming his guitar wearing nothing but his underwear and a pair Cowboy boots. As the sun went down, New York changed to a magical city bright and beautiful.

The quest

❖ ❖ ❖

This is the story of a man I met as an eight-year-old back at my home town decades ago.

He was song writer, lyricist, singer, poet, filmmaker, a gifted person who influenced generations of people in the Indian subcontinent. Even today, in my sunset years when I look back, I feel indebted to him for his vision, wisdom, love for humanity chiselled in my heart which I was privileged to follow. His name was Dr Bhupen Hazarika.

His songs are loaded with love for universal brotherhood, justice and empathy. Some of his heart rendering lyrics, I still hum on my lonely moments for guidance and inspiration. They say, "Never underestimate the power of dreams and influence of human spirit", for me and many of my generation he remains supreme. Sadly, his songs have not yet arrived the shores of England. I tried to translate some of his music for you today, at the risk of mutilating the beauty and rhythms of lyrics he crafted.

Bhupen Hazarika was the eldest son of a school teacher with ten children. The country was riddled with poverty, lack of basic amenities, hardship every single day. That did not stop him looking at the future. He dreamt of an equitable world. He pursued his studies and finally he did a doctorate from Columbia University in USA. There he met Paul Robson, a prominent civil rights activist who influenced him in writing lyrics. Paul Robson's song 'ole man river' was one of the first songs he adapted to Indian scenario, "We are in the same boat brother" which opened the eyes of Indian youths of the day to think in an international perspective the disparity of rich and poor over the world. His personal life was punctuated by a failed marriage, lack of support in academic life, struggle to make his mark in national musical establishment. Yet he never gave up his dream of a better world. Finally, he won accolades, highest awards of India, Bangladesh. Japan awarded him with the highest award for International film production.

Today Indians are at the helm of World's most prestigious institutions e.g. Google, Microsoft, Mastercard and many are top leaders of international industries, universities, politics, literature, space science. UK is undoubtedly a beneficiary of long time Indian association.

A relationship of mutual love and respect.

He wrote a song named:

> "I am a wanderer
> The world having embraced me as its own, I have forgotten my own home
> I've become a wanderer from the land of Brahmaputra, I visited the mighty Mississippi, I saw the beautiful Volga on my way
> From Ottawa through Austria I arrived in Paris
> From Ellora I brought brilliant paints and gave it to Chicago city
> I heard the music of Galib, sitting inside the minaret in Tashkent
> Sitting at Mark Twain's tombstone I thought of Gorki the great
> Again, and again my lust for wonder made the road my home.

That's why I am a wanderer.
Though my wandering appears to be aimless, I travel with intention:
Wherever I go I soak my mind with local colours.
I have seen countless rows of tall buildings touching the sky
Under their shadow I saw many homeless dies.
I have seen endless groves of roses and jasmine flowers in millions
I have seen beautiful buds withering away to dust."

Bhupen engraved his message of universal love before John Lennon composed his song "Imagine" in 1971. Souls of millions of Indians still reverberates with the rhythm of his songs.

May be his ultimate dream of love and universal brotherhood will come true for all of us someday, without prejudice of race, religion, political persuasion.

That will be the day of heaven on earth.

Bhupen Hazarika died on 5 November 2011. His last wish was to scatter his ash on river Brahmaputra, the "Ole Man River" who was the silent witness of all his failures and successes in life.

His funeral was attended by half a million mourners, only second to Mahatma Gandhi's funeral in India.

He was just an ordinary person with huge contributions that inspired masses with a dream to make the world a better place.

Triptych of 'Lockdown'

❖ ❖ ❖

The Inception
In the Winter of 2019, a subtle invisible life form, a novel virus appeared in the city of Wuhan.
A curse to Mankind without warning, death without discrimination.
Mankind survived many such viruses before.
This was the most virulent of all viral affliction.
Millions died, no one knows how to abate such an annihilation.

A Visit to Hospital:
I woke up this morning with a mixed bag of emotions.
My mind was on a journey, trying to find out how this battle is fought?
I arrived at the gate of the hospital, walked in to witness the battle between death and being alive.
Lines of people filled the halls and cubicles in every corner available
The victims of an emergency never seen before.
I saw something amazing for the first time in my life, mass death and battle to survive.
Doctors trying to save life, some nursing, doing their best to keep people alive.
There was an old man who could hardly stand, asked if he can swap his bed
… for the dying man laid on a chair.

I saw an expert in Palliative Medicine helping the dying man.
Gasping for his breath for the very last time.
... I bowed my head to those who gave their lives for our sake so that we can survive.

The 'lockdown'
Life under our loss of freedom, confusion and fear of unknown, gets harder to carry on.
Still no signs of retreat of our arch enemy the virus with crowns.
I looked through the window of my lounge, it's beautiful sunny day.
I know millions have suffered; many have died. We shall and will not give up.
Until we win this battle again, life goes on, so will the joy of life.

Values of changing time

❖ ❖ ❖

Have you heard of Dukeries? May be not. I spent forty years of my life in a little town called Worksop in Dukeries not far from Sheffield. Once favoured as country retreat by many of the Dukes and Lords. On occasions I met one or two titled families who happened to be my patients. I got to know some of their staff well as they were regular patients.

Now this story is about Mr James Murphy, head gamekeeper of one such estate, Dukeries House. One day on my return home I found Mr Murphy sitting at my kitchen breakfast table with a glass of whisky talking to my wife. He smiled at me warmly, my wife said, "See what Mr Murphy got for us for dinner".

The reason for Mr Murphy's visit was to tell my wife that I did something for his teenage daughter for which the Duchess sent some pheasants to thank me for. I was not sure what exactly I did to earn my free goodies, none the less we were pleased to receive her gifts. Later I remembered, I sent young Anna for a scan for intermittent back pain, just to reassure her (and me) that there was no sinister cause to worry.

To my surprise the scan report came back advising that the back pain might have been due to a suspected tumour. I arranged for urgent hospital admission and she went through a successful major operation. The story eventually reached the Duchess, and we were added to the list of recipients for a free turkey at Christmas time. Mr Murphy enjoyed chatting to my wife and her generous offer of my malt whisky when he visited our house.

Over a period of time we came to learn about the historical connection of the Murphy family and that of Lord Dukeries, owners of the estate for generations.

James Murphy was the fourth generation of head gamekeeper in the estate. He came to work as a stable boy at the age of fourteen when his granddad bought him to Dukeries House from Ireland. Granddad told him to be loyal, honest, above all faithful to his Masters, the Greats and Good and Nobles, chosen to rule over the world by God. James promised, he would keep his word and serve his masters as best as he could.

In return for his loyalty James and family had the privilege of a free grace and favour house designed by famous architect James Paine, surrounded by a garden, landscaped by Capability Brown.

One day James invited me to his house, I saw a painting of his grandfather, red in the face, wearing a hunter's hat, in traditional legwear, thigh-high shooting socks and boots. A sign of respect by the staff and masters of the estate.

James looked sad when he recalled a time when clients had class, dressed formally, there were great parties, music, gaiety and dance, *hanky-panky* and etiquette. There were many secrets too, that can't be divulged. Those were the golden days of high society. His pay was not much, but tips were very generous.

He took me for a ride around the gardens and the wood, a Grecian unpretentious house, reminder of a distant glorious past.

After the tour James took me to the far end of the estate and showed the graveyard filled with long gone ancestors. James pointed to a small plot of land and said His Lordship told him, "This is where I want to be buried, my doctor told me that my cancer has spread, you have been close to me more than sixty years, please take care of my wife and children when I die". Soon he passed away.

I looked around, head stones bore the names of Earls, Lords, Generals, Knights, Colonial Governors from the 17th century till date. Here lie the witnesses of the Britain's voyages through history.

James did his last shoot and retired yesterday.

I saw a confused old man with misty eyes: a misfit, his values, noble and selfless service to his masters now feel like hallucinations trapped in a time capsule.

I gave him a hug, wished him well, ... said Goodbye.

A visit like no other

❖ ❖ ❖

One autumn we visited "The Hermitage" museum in St Petersburg in Russia. The museum was founded by Empress Catherine the Great in 1764. It was recommended to us by one of our friends as one of the top destinations to visit in the world. He told us that the whole museum is a huge complex of six buildings of palaces of Russian emperors and contains 3 million pieces of arts. We pre-organised our tickets and booked our tour in advance as advised by our travel agent. It was indeed a good decision as we noticed a great number of visitors that morning in long queues.

We were received by our guide at the impressive entrance of the Winter palace. After a bit of push and shove we were able to get inside the entrance hall of that huge neoclassical building. Because of the cacophony of multiple languages, we were unable to hear clearly our Russian guide explaining about our day's plans and various important exhibits. She had a Russian accent, spoke in halting English and gesticulated with her hands to navigate through the crowded halls.

Although "Hermitage" sounds like a humble place, that's a misnomer in reality. Once we were inside the hall, the grace, beauty and the enormity of the buildings briefly numbed my senses. We were given a map of the palace and were warned by the guide not to stray away. She told us that this museum is the second largest museum in the world, after "Le Louvre" in Paris (we have been to Le Louvre before). This building is interlinked to four others, a total of 400 rooms on three floors. She also told us that if we want to see all the exhibits, it will take one 25 years to complete the tour of this place. Before our tour she gave us a map each, highlighting the interesting exhibits. She pointed to us the staircase to upper floors made of marble, granite laced with gold ribbons. She told us the exhibits were left untouched and in their original places since the beginning when that palace was used as private quarter of the royal family. We saw spectacular Russian and European arts adorning tall walls. A collection of Michelangelo's sculptures, paintings by Raphael, Tintoretto, Caravaggio was packed with masses of people. When I turned my eyes, I saw Vandyke, Ruben, Rembrandt starring into my eyes.

A feast of beauty that overwhelmed my senses with disbelief and exhilarated till this day.

As we went from floor to floor, my mind bedazzled with excitement. The Peacock Clock made in England 200 years ago adorned with three golden mechanical birds in a gilded garden drew a large crowd around its vicinity. While we were there the clock began to chime music when the owl turns its head. Then the peacock gracefully turns its neck and lifts its tail slowly before quickly turning around to display its fan of golden feathers. We spent nearly three hours walking floor to floor.

After a while we were taken to another part of the building complex through the palace gardens designed in a formal rectangular pattern. Soon we arrived at the private quarters where Catherine the great (founder of museum in 1764) had her bedroom. It was an opulent room, not very big with an attached washroom. The guide pointed our attention towards a secret passage. She then smiled coyly and said, "This was used by Catherine's lovers".

The lady behind me gasped, "What? more than one?"

The guide nodded her head and said, "Yes, many more than that, she had many more young lovers over a period of time". Then she raised her left hand and showed full five fingers, soon she added the other five fingers of the right hand, making it ten, and said, "Add another ten, now you know, she had more than twenty young lovers."

"Yes", she nodded her head again to confirm her statement.

On my way back to the hotel, I was thinking about of all the great painters who created those beautiful works of art, "The Return of the Prodigal Son" by Rembrandt, Leonardo's "the Madonna Litta", Van Gogh's "Thatched cottages", Gauguin's "The woman holding fruit" and many more treasures collected by the Royals over three centuries under one roof.

I still got the map and the guide book to "The Hermitage" on my bookshelf to look up from time to time.

Whispering stones and weeping trees

Angkor Wat

❖ ❖ ❖

A travelogue

You may or may not be familiar with this place, if you look up the globe, it is situated at 13°41N, 103°85E in eastern Cambodia, the land of the Khmer people. A place in tropical rain forest, lush green, fertile, abundance of nature's bountiful gifts and yet cursed with a sad history. Over the centuries hordes of invaders ruled its people and homegrown tyrants leaving behind a legacy of death, gore and destruction. Recorded history bears the scars of Thai invasion, followed by Vietnamese, Portuguese, French, Japanese, and others. Finally, independence arrived in 1955. However, peace was still a distant dream, Khmer Rouge the communist homegrown party took over the government in 1955. Theirs was a regime associated with untold misery, genocide, disease, starvation and forced labour. We were told two million people, 24% of the local population died – the killing fields of our time. At last peace arrived in 1979. Soon Angkor Wat, the hidden jewel on earth became accessible to the wide world.

Angkor Wat is the largest complex of monuments spreading over 162 hectors (400 square kilometres) consisting of 100s of temples, hydraulic structures, communication routes, moats built between 802–1220 AD. This is called humankind's most astounding and endearing architectural achievement, surpassing that of the Pyramids in Egypt, the Gardens of Babylon and the Taj-mahal in India.

Thanks to French explorer Henry Mouhat, in 1860 his rediscovery of the neglected temple complex was brought to the world's attention. In recent times UNESCO declared the temple complex a world heritage site and conservation started gradually, restoring the neglected ruins. In 2017, 2.5 million people visited the complex.

On a fine beautiful morning of 22 September 2018, we were picked up from our hotel in a coach by our friendly, knowledgeable Khmer guide. As we approached the countryside the scenery was that of a rural fields of rice green, tarmacked main roads, narrow mud tracked side roads, few half-built brick houses with tin roofs, old village hutments on stiletto. Every house seemed to have a vegetable patch, tall betel nut trees, coconut groves, cluster of shops with thatched roof and bamboo walls, pigs roaming freely, dogs and cows lazing leisurely, people chatting to neighbours in a relaxed manner. Although there were plenty of billboards advertising Japanese T.V.s, Korean Mobile phones, Western lady's beauty products, I suspect for the locals those belonged to a different world. An illusion of a fast-changing world.

We arrived at Angkor Wat at about 10 am. The parking lots were already full of tourists. Soon we were surrounded by a group of kids trying to sell us various souvenirs, guide books, fans, water, nuts etc. A little girl, maybe 10 year or so suddenly appeared with a camera in a tatty torn frock, sad demeanour and took photos of us. She said photos cost $3/each. I bought one of her photos. The Guide was not happy, he said, she will only get pennies for spending all day taking pictures which is to help poor family,

it's the organized gangs who benefit from her labour. Finally, we walked inside the temple complex. It was an awe-inspiring spectacular sight. We entered via the south gate flanked by 54 devils and gods locked in a tag of war pulling a huge snake. We saw lines of elephants, along the 350-meter-long terrace, leading through the citadel to Bayan. Suddenly I felt a spooky feeling, a pair of giant eyes watching me, heart missed a beat. Then I saw the great Buddha sitting cross-legged in meditation. At Ta Prahm temple a mighty old overgrown majestic tree stands in silence with huge roots. On my east, I saw a female deity. Our eight-hour tour was like a moment of time to absorb thousand years of antiquity. There are thousands of beautiful artefacts curved in stone, old trees, moats, old buildings scattered all over the landscapes, done by sheer power of imagination and brute muscle power in the name of God – Vishnu. I was humbled by the enormity of such an achievement by those people thousands of years ago. But I did not see any acknowledgement of all those labourers, estimated at 300,000 in number who slaved for the glory of the king and country. My heart sank when the guide showed us the terrace where Pol Pot and his cronies shot dead thousands of their own countryman suspected of harbouring capitalist ideals. The guide pointed out the bullet holes of massacres that look fresh, it was in 1970s. I thought about the tag of war mural seen earlier. I asked the guide if I can come back at a quiet time, he hesitated and said may be not a good idea, people say in the quiet of the night the stones whisper and the trees cry. This place is haunted, some nights a white owl cries to remind locals to light a candle for the souls of the dead in limbo.

I have visited many parts of the world; nothing compares to Angkor Wat.

Hidden jewels of the Lake District

❖ ❖ ❖

One summer we decided to explore the wilderness of the Lake District. Explorers included me, my wife and couple of our friends from the south of England. Criteria of the location was to find a place with low number of tourists, remote, comfortable, favourable for walking for amateur hill walkers.

After much search we decided to visit a little place between Wasdale and Eskdale hidden away in the hills of Cumbria's western fells.

After a long drive through the narrow tortuous roads, passing through the central Lakeland via Hardknott and Wrynose passes, we finally arrived at our destination – The "Irton Hall", snuggled cosily between the hills in the Cumbrian countryside.

As we approached the remote place, we saw a very old sprawling red brick building, extensive grounds surrounding the house and a few very old trees.

On the first day of arrival, we were very tired. Daylight disappeared soon after we arrived. There were only a handful of guests that night, we had to get our dinner fairly early that day as the kitchen staff wanted to catch the last bus back home before darkness descended behind the hills in the Western sky.

To our dismay there was no other eatery to choose for a drink in the vicinity of the hotel. Next morning, after a sumptuous breakfast that included sausage, black pudding, hash brown, tomato, mushrooms, beans, and a choice of either fried, poached or scrambled eggs, we went around the hotel compound. Soon the history of that house began to unfold of that was once a great place where history was made over five centuries, from Norman conquest through to Henry VI, who during the Wars of roses, came seeking shelter at Irton Hall, but was declined by the then Yorkist owner of the manor. Because Henry was a supporter of Lancastrians. So good old Henry spent the night under the great oak tree in the ground of the manor. That oak is still in its place, they call it "the Kings Oak" (now 1000 year old).

Oliver Cromwell was among other famous visitors during the mid-17th century.

The Irton family played important part while history was made during the crusades. The long history of Irton family *came* to an end in 1866 when Samuel Irton died.

Mrs Irton tried to destroy the family history (reasons are not known to me), current owners are trying to revive the glory of another time.

First Easter

❖ ❖ ❖

It was a golden morning, with glitters on the grass
I saw my little granddaughter chasing a little bird
She crouched upon the ground to touch a little flower.
The joy of velvety softness filled her with wonder.
She saw two little squirrels, chasing each other
She smiled happily when they looked at her with their big black eyes
Her mum and grandma joined us
To hunt for Easter eggs
We had lots of fun looking under the hedge.
In all that excitement she dropped one of her eggs.
If ever there were a spring day so perfect
I would release all creatures trapped in a cage
Like in a walled prison confused in a daze.
I looked at the glass globe on my study table
Where a peacock is entrapped pleading
"Please let me be free".
I wish one day he too will be happy and free
To fly away like a little bee.

A Christmas gift

(from long gone past)

❖ ❖ ❖

Yesterday, I brought down our Christmas decorations and Christmas cards. Before I threw them away, I looked at those Christmas cards one more time. All those cards carried the wishful thought ...

> "Wishing you the very best of health and joy and peace!
> Love and good wishes for a happy new year."

Last Christmas, there had been no parties, no family reunion, no exchange of gifts (except by post), no hugs. The dark shadows of ominous clouds of an invisible enemy (pandemic of COVID-19) robbed us of normality.

This morning my wife gave me another sad news, two of my class mates passed away in last two weeks.

The word "Hope" is playing in my mind.

Many years ago, I attended a course on "Positive Psychology", they told us hope is a state of mind based on a sense of successful goal-directed thinking. One has to construct specific strategies to arrive at their chosen goals.

Hope endures life challenging events and gives us the strength to be optimistic and bring us positivity. Sometime out of desperation greatness is born. Here is a story of a Scottish man, Allan Octavian Hume who was a civil servant in British India (during and after the massacres of Sepoy mutiny 1857) and changed the destiny of millions of Indian people. Although he was an instrument of the British administration, he was unhappy with the extravagance and exploitations by his own countrymen and deprivation of native people. At the age of fifty-four he retired and plunged himself into local politics of the day. He became part of the first Indian political party, National Congress in India.

He was convinced that the way to improve the lots of Indians was through democracy. He organized the Indian National Congress on the *Christmas of 1885*. He took the initiative to personally write a letter to every living Indian graduate of Calcutta University.

His letter said –

> "To those – ... who love India and her children ... but real work must be done by the people of the country themselves ... if fifty men cannot be found with sufficient power of self-sacrifice, sufficient love for and pride in their country, sufficient genuine and unselfish patriotism to take the initiative and if needs be devoting the rest of their lives to the Cause – then there is no hope for India. Her sons must and will remain mere humble and helpless instruments of foreign rulers ..."

The clarion call Mr Hume made that day inspired Indians to bring an end to colonial slavery and reignited the hope and dreams for a free nation.

Around that time European community rejected the idea of liberal humanitarian legislation for the local population. It was due to Mr Hume's firm belief that repression must come to an end. He took the responsibility to serve the Indian National Congress for 22 years as its general secretary after his retirement.

Post Script:
In 1894 Mr Hume returned to London.

On 31 July in the year 1912, Mr Hume died in London.

On his grave stone at Brookwood Cemetery the following inscription states his lifetime's ambitions –

> "Here", after asking the subjugated Indians "Are ye or are ye freeman, ye who grovel in the shade?". He proclaimed rousingly, "In your own hands rest the issues! By themselves are nations made".

Today India is the biggest democracy in the world, a secular democracy of 1.3 billion people.

Thank you, thank you Mr Allan Octavian Hume, thanks for your Christmas gift to a nation, the courage to hope and dream of being a freeman.

India became an independent nation on 15 August 1947.

Mr Hume's other great contribution was as an ornithologist of international reputation on Birds of India.

On 31 July 1973 India issued a commemorative postage stamp in honour of Allan Octavian Hume.

The Kipling stories

❖ ❖ ❖

Rudy (Rudyard) from Rye, does it a ring a bell in your memory?

Yes, Rudyard Kipling. He made Rye famous after he settled in Rye in Sussex in England. He wrote "Jungle Book", a classic for every child that inspired generations of children to fire up their imaginations, a book that immortalised him as a story teller and made him the youngest Englishman to win a Nobel prize in literature.

But was he the original story teller about the jungle boy and his adventures?

Maybe, maybe not. He himself confessed, when he was a child in Bombay, "in the afternoon heats before we took our sleep, she (the ayah) Meeta would tell us stories and sing Indian nursery songs, now all forgotten, and we were sent into the dining-room after we had been dressed, with caution, speak English now to Papa and Mama. So, one spoke 'English' haltingly translated out of the vernacular idiom that one thought and dreamt in".

However, this happy time ended when Rudyard was sent back to England at the age of five. This experience left Rudyard confused, a young man without a clear understanding of his sense of "belonging" or his "alienation", like his protagonist Mowgli who was a human brought up as a wolf-cub by a wolf mother, belonging to neither.

There is a place called Peshawar (now in Pakistan), if you happen to be there, please pay a visit to meet Mahammad Nassim, the last of the story tellers where the Silk Road from China was located on the edge of the Khyber Pass. Where stories from one generation to the next were passed on at Qissa Khawni (Story teller's Bazaar). People still share those stories from long gone past and folklores that enriched the history of humanity.

After I wrote this story about Rudyard Kipling, I phoned my friend Rudy. I asked him, "Is Rudy short for Rudyard?"

He said, "No. It is German for son of a wolf".

"What about Rudyard?"

He replied, "Rudyard is the name of a lake in Staffordshire, Kipling's parents fell in love around that beautiful lake in their courting days. So, they named their first child Rudyard."

I wonder, Rudy was it Kipling's pet name?

Did Rudyard know that a son of a wolf was called Rudy?

Was an Indian jungle boy Mowgli (adopted son of a wolf), a self-portrayal of Rudyard's subconscious alter ego?

The Hawley

❖ ❖ ❖

I was waiting this afternoon for a mail from my friend Lesley. She forwarded a few photographs of old houses ravaged by time. On closer look I still can see remnants of their glorious past, now ravaged by time, depredation, waste and devastation and abandonment. It made me sad, my thoughts re-winded and arrived at my childhood.

There were once three beautiful houses in that landscape with extended manicured gardens. A place once owned by my great-grandfather. The one that is still just standing belonged to my grandfather and that was where my mum gave birth to me and two of my siblings. Now empty, desolate, on the verge of collapse, once an opulent Hawley.

The word Hawley in Assamese (my mother tongue) means a mansion with a big compound, usually of historical significance.

I was told that my granddad built that house in the design of the local king's Palace which he used to visit as a child accompanying his father. After the kingdom came to an end following Internal dispute of the Royal family, betrayal and finally led to repeated invasions by hostile neighbouring kingdom, the king abandoned the town. He sold his property to my great grandfather. On his death the property was divided among his three boys. In due course their children inherited those properties but with the change of time and more mouths to feed, they pulled down those big houses. The only one that's still standing is the one my grandfather built. Over the time that house got neglected as no one wants to own a "white elephant".

On my last visit I went for a walk around my birth place and remembered the tales of its glorious past.

Once in that compound lived the local Governor of the Ahom Kingdom, that was the house where my great uncle raised India's National flag defying British rule (and served long prison sentence for his bravery). One of my widowed aunts wrote poems to encourage nonviolent struggle for Indian independence encouraged by Mahatma Gandhi, Indian independence leaders planned and dreamt of being a free nation.

Once that house turns to dust, part of proud history of that land will vanish for ever.

Indeed, it will always be a proud memory which I shall never forget.

Missing pages

❖ ❖ ❖

I grew up in a small town in India many years ago. For the children, there was a playground which was overcrowded most winter days. Summer days were long, hot and sweaty and we were confined to our houses. Once Dad left for work, mum kept herself busy, after her bath and prayers, she would take her breakfast, read the daily newspapers. Then she would instruct the cook about our lunch. After lunch she would be in her bed for an hour to rest.

For me the most boring time of the day.

In my boredom I used to rummage through Dad's Library. One day I found a slim little book where I discovered a picture postcard tucked between its pages. A picture of a narrow sunken cobbled street in a city called Pompeii in Italy.

The name of the book was "An unrecorded chapter in the Political evolution of Assam", authored by P.K. Baruah.

The author wrote in the introduction, "I wrote the first part of this narrative mainly from my memory and remnants of a moth-eaten Diary within seven days".

Here is what he wrote in his diary:

19 June 1919
"They (the members of the Association) mooted the question of sending a two men delegation to London. The committee emphasised the importance of the mission, as failure to act decisively will cause irreversible damage to the country and

to the future generations. (there was a plot to assign Assam to Pakistan). They nominated me as one of the two-man delegation. Considering the grave situations, I volunteered to plead our cause to Lord Selbourne in London.

July 1919

My brother-in-law (the other delegation member) and I went to Thomas Cook & Son in Calcutta and we booked our berths in *S.S. Kaiser Hind*, a very beautiful ship, 11,000 tonnage for 29 July from Bombay. In Calcutta we ordered at Whiteways for up-to-date London Fashion suits and Dinner jackets etc. On the train to Bombay, a French man joined us. He said he got his English girlfriend into "trouble" and was on a police warrant, he was doing a runner back to his home in France.

4 August

We arrived at Aden. Walked a short distance and saw some camels, bought a few melons and packs of Turkish cigars.

7 August

We passed through the Suez Canal to Port Said, saw a great statue of Count Lessep (Developer of Suez Canal).

14 August 19

"Arrived in Naples. Joined a day trip to Pompeii. The City was destroyed completely when Mount Vesuvius erupted in AD 79. Recently (1911) they excavated the ruined city and visitors are arriving in droves. We saw many narrow sunken cobbled streets and saw a bakery of Roman times. I bought a post card to send home when I arrive in London."

After the entry dated 14 August, the chronology of the places he visited and details of the diary were less than precise (may be due to failing memories, or missing pages swallowed by the moths. It is possible he was tied up with the serious business of saving his country from impending danger of political espionage and subversion plotted by the enemies of his people.)

After a lot of hard work and sustained efforts the delegation convinced the British Parliament that Assam belonged to India.

The author also recorded a few other amusing and humorous incidents in his diaries.

When I visited Pompeii a few years ago, the city looked the same since that post card was sent to my Dad many years ago.

I felt a sense of Déjà vu of the old post card, a place in silence, desolation, forlorn feelings, without a tree or a bird. Although the dry bare stone walls are still standing in silence, I saw patches of green grass and Japanese Ivy creeping up on those walls.

There are plaster cast displays of many of the victims of that disaster ever since Mount Vesuvius erupted in AD79.

One can see the agony of death written on the faces of those people, eerily preserved, reminding us of the poignant past of the old devastated city.

Post Script: P.K. Baruah and his Brother in law's mission to the British parliament was a resounding success. Assam remained part of India after India became an independent Nation.

The old man died on 25 November 1958.

The man with a foreign hat

❖ ❖ ❖

The first time I met Ivan was when he came to pick me up from home to Heathrow airport a few years ago. At that time, I was working for an International pharmaceutical company as an expert clinical adviser. My job entailed attending International meetings and arrange clinical trials. One of the perks of the job was travelling to various countries, all paid for by the company I worked for.

Ivan was a very impressive man, 6ft 6in. tall, big built, spoke to me in a strong Russian accent "gut morning, my name is Ivan, your driver", he said.

He loaded my cases and we were off. Once we settled down, he told me that he is Russian. He had been in England for the last two years. Soon I realised that he likes to chat while driving to break the monotony and to help him improve his spoken English.

He volunteered the information that he was a retired commander (komvzvoda) of the Russian Army. I did notice Ivan wearing a Russian Army fur hat when he came to my door. By the time we were off, he carefully folded his hat and put it in the glove box.

Ivan asked me where I was from. When I said I was from India, he smiled and said "*Hindi –Russi bhai bhai*", meaning the old Indian slogan, "Indians and Russians are brothers". Once we had to learn that phrase by heart at school as some top Russian dignitary was visiting our town. Ivan said, he was one of the military security men accompanying the big shot at that time. We had a good laugh and enjoyed each other's company. From then on Ivan was my chauffeur for most of my trips abroad. We became rather friendly over the time.

I asked Ivan how he ended up in England? He said, after USSR came to an end, he moved to Ukraine on his retirement and changed his citizenship. Now he got his EU passport and decided to move to England. He told me; in Russia his pension was around £4,500/per year. He managed with that money as he had no family and he was never married. His only family was his sister Daria who was a lecturer at the university and one nephew Maskin still at school. He said, he liked England. Once a cheeky young driver called him a liar for making up stories to get attention. Recently another challenged him to a fight to prove he was a genuine Army combatant.

Ivan told him, "Look I am trained to kill, not to fight for fun. You may be a better boxer than me and will probably win, but you will end up in a coffin".

I asked him which part of Russia he was from. Ivan said he is a Cossack. They live in the steppe area of the North Black Sea in southern Russia and Ukraine. Some even moved to Western Siberia. He said, on his last visit home he was presented with a Usanka fur hat by his old friends and pointed his finger to the glove box in the car.

Half way to the airport Ivan's phone rang, it was from Dimitry his old friend. Ivan apologised and asked me if it was all right to talk in Russian.

I said "carry on".

Conversation between Dimitry and Ivan started well, like polite greetings between two old friends. Soon I noticed a change of tone from intimate to earnest mingling names like, Kuznetsov,

Kirov, Burusevic floating in and out of their discussion. I could hear Dimitry raising his voice, stuttering like a machine gun fire, shouting in anger. He paused briefly, said something formally like an order, then put the phone down. Ivan's mood change was dramatic, from relaxed to tense, then capricious in a brief period of time.

We had no further conversation between us till we arrived at the Airport. I could physically feel a sense of permafrost seeping in inside the car.

On arrival at the Airport, I handed over a tenner to Ivan, saying as usual, "This is for your nephew Maskin", he did not reply.

On my return to Heathrow after a week I could not find Ivan. I saw another driver holding a card with my name written on it. I asked him where was Ivan? He said, "I don't know him, I came to collect you on short notice".

That night sitting in my lounge, I was watching BBC World News when there was a "Breaking News" flash: "Russian warship fleet moved into English Channel when UK was distracted by National virus epidemic, fleet including aircraft carrier General Kuznetsov and six other battleships this morning".

I rang to Ivan's Taxi office to find out why he did not come to meet me. The lady said "I am new here. I don't know all the drivers; I can see you are in the list of our frequent flyers." I told her Ivan is a big man, a Russian with a Cossack hat. She asked me to wait so that she could talk to her manager. On her return she told me, "Manager said he knew Ivan very well. This morning someone from Home Office came looking for him, there were a few more public enquiries, may be from MI5, could be CIA or it could be Russian FSB, no one knows, where he has gone".

The man in a foreign hat left town.

Dr Freud and the rabbit

❖ ❖ ❖

The morning after Dr Freud and his friend Dr Jung had a lovely meal of rabbit stew, something strange happened to both experts of Psychoanalysis. Facts became more confusing on the breakfast table when the cook insisted that the dinner was definitely that of a rabbit meat, not of a man with dissociative *fugue* state of mind masquerading as a rabbit. When Dr Freud tried to focus on his boiled egg he saw a many *hued* rabbit sitting, *morn* and *scared*, *sank* in a huge *orange* egg cup dangling his *hind* legs.

Suddenly Dr Jung screamed in joy shouting, "Look, look, here is a nude wearing a tight *quoif* on a rude *oxen*".

Both elderly men realised, things were not all right, decided to go for walk in *the town*.

Dr Jung liked instrumental music, and saw a beautiful *Lyre* harp in the music shop around the corner. There was a price tag of £200/+VAT, T reminded him to visit the toilet. So they changed their minds, walked through the *bay* to drink a pint of Mikkeler Spontan beer. Soon they got drunk, lost their *hats*, wetted their *suits*, walked out of toilet with *zips* down like two clueless *plebs*.

A policeman who was watching their antics, walked to them and said: "I have been watching you two, time to pay a visit to the *Jail*".

Dr Freud tried to distract the policeman, shouting, "Look, look, there are foxes all over the place, run, run, run".

Investigations confirmed both the psychiatrists were experimenting on psychedelic effects of luminescent glow warm insects from New Zealand or was it the magic mushroom?

The way we were

❖ ❖ ❖

Lucy was feeling edgy and panicky after being beaten up by a gang.

It had been a difficult time since she moved out of her foster parent's home after turning eighteen. Thankfully with the help of social services, she had found a bedsit where she met Gemma. They got on well and Lucy joined the college course and was looking forward to a normal life. Memories of past abusive chaotic life, her anxiety, loneliness, feelings of abandonment were now bearable but still hurt.

One night when Gemma got home, she found Lucy distressed with bruises on her bleeding swollen face.

Gemma asked her, "Oh my God, what happened to you, was it an accident?".

Lucy said, "No, I was beaten up", after a pause she told Gemma, "Jason and his gang had been pestering me for the last few weeks, today I lost my temper when they called me a slut. I warned them not to call me like that, they thought it was hilarious. One of them grabbed me from the back and pulled me down. I panicked, I thought they were going to rape me, I screamed. No one came to help me, no one seemed to care. I saw a face closing in, touching my face, he was holding my arm. Finally, I head butted him as hard as I could when blood dripped down from his face and from my gum. The other two took photos of me up-skirting and put them on line with my name in it. That's when I flipped, I punched, his face and got beaten up. I am not going to let them get away, just wait and see, they will get it back."

That night Lucy was unable to sleep, she finally dozed off in the early morning hours. Once again, she had that nasty old dream. The smell of alcohol, stale cigarette, a phantasm (that's what my Doctor called it) revisited once again. she saw the ugly face of her uncle closing in, Lucy shouted, tried to resist but to no avail. She woke up in a jolt, mumbling "I am eighteen now, I will take revenge".

Gemma walked in and asked, "Are you alright? You must have been in a lot of pain; I could hear you groan last night. I'll bring some paracetamol when I come home tonight. I made you some sandwiches for lunch, and I'll try to phone you when I get a break. Maybe you can ask Brenda if she can pop in for a chat."

Lucy phoned her foster mum Brenda and told her what happened in college. Brenda was furious, she said, "Don't let them get away, next time grab their balls and kick their arse or I will sort them out", after a pause Brenda said, "Look love, you are a clever girl, you did well with three Cs and one D in your GCSE. Work hard and get your qualifications, you may go to Uni, some day."

After talking to Brenda Lucy felt better.

Next day Gemma suggested, "Let's go to the pub, and chill out tonight".

It was a nice autumn day, relaxed, with warm and friendly people around. Lucy felt happy. There was a young man showing off his new red motor bike revving the engine, letting the clutch out until the front wheel lifted. Soon a bunch of kids were watching him when he dared them to sit on the back of his bike. No one volunteered. He called Lucy to join him and soon they were off.

Next morning Lucy told Gemma, "His name was Ron, and he lives in the next village. We talked a lot last night and I told him about the gang beating me up".

Lucy told Gemma that Ron got cross and said, "Leave it to me, I shall sort them out". He phoned his mates and called them out.

Next day, seven of them came to our college and gave them a good hiding to teach them a lesson and told them to leave me alone. Ron told me that one of the gang members is with the local motorbike chapter. No one will dare to upset me any longer, I am safe from now on.

One day Ron took Lucy to meet his brother Dan. Although Ron and Dan were twins, Lucy found out that in a strange way they were very close to each other but mentally they were world apart. When their mum died, Ron insisted on selling her home and taking the money to buy a Triumph motorbike, but Dan wanted to keep the house and raised a mortgage to payoff for Ron's share.

Lucy noticed, Dan was conscientious, soft spoken and serious, while Ron was excitable, adventurous and quick-tempered. One day Dan told Lucy that their Dad was an American G.I. who came to England in 1942. He was a generous man and brought candy, Coca-cola, cigarettes, nylon stockings to parties where their mum met him.

Soon they fell in love. Later they found out that Dad was like many other G.I.s who only wanted a good time, women, parties and fun. When the twins were about ten years old, their Dad decided to pack his bag and returned home. He gave enough money to buy the terraced house to their mum. Mum used to say Ron got his American genes and Dan got his mum's English genes.

Ron always wanted to dress up as a tough man in black leather on a powerful motorbike, road romance, to belong to a motorbike club.

Lucy noticed Dan was totally different, wearing a pair of plain trousers and a long sleeve shirt. He had many books, a CD player with stacks of records scattered all over the room. She felt there was a peaceful serene ambience in his house. There was a figure of an Asian man on his desk. Lucy asked, "Who was that man?"

Dan said, "He is Buddha, the founder of Buddhism". Ron did tell her that Dan had changed his faith to Buddhism after reading a book by Dalai Lama, "The Art of Happiness".

One day Lucy told Gemma that she was splitting up from Ron. This was because, Ron had been out of his mind and roughing her up.

He lost his job after a fight with his boss and was expelled from his motorbike chapter for knifing a brother biker. On his return home, he blamed Lucy for flirting with the other biker who called her a slut and him a fluke, that's what made him lose his temper.

Next morning Lucy packed her bag and moved in with Dan. Dan called her in, saw the bruises and gently washed off the blood. He made her a hot drink and asked what has gone wrong between her and Ron. Later that night he ran her a hot bath, cooked a nice dinner and moved to the sofa in the lounge offering the bed to Lucy.

Three nights later Lucy asked Dan to join her on his bed, it did not feel right.

Next morning, she phoned Ron to tell him that she did not love him no more.

Dan and Lucy were gradually settling down to a routine of daily life. Dan usually will wake up early to go to work while

Lucy would stay in bed late and take it easy. One morning after Dan had gone to work, Lucy was sitting with her morning cup of tea, the doorbell rang. Lucy opened the door. There were two policemen, one was old, the other was young. The older one politely asked if they can come in, Lucy said "yes".

The Sergeant apologised and asked if she was Lucy. She nodded. The officer said, "I am sorry, I got some bad news. Ron was found dead last night in his flat. It looks like suicide. He left two letters, one for you and one for his brother."

Lucy opened her letter.

Ron wrote, "I know I did it wrong. I could not take it any longer. At school they taunted me calling me a bastard and my mum a tart. They did not like our Dad because he was African American.

When I met you, I thought we could be happy, as you too, had a hard time growing up. You said, you had a dream, maybe someday you will find someone who will love you and you will love him in return. A little house, two beautiful kids, a pet was all you wanted in life. Believe me, I loved you from the bottom of my heart. I thought, one day we shall build a home between us and be together for the rest of our lives."

Lucy, she just sat there, the only thing that came to her mind was the first sentence of her text book – Anna Karenina: "All happy families are alike; each unhappy family is unhappy in its own way."

The vigil

❖ ❖ ❖

Part I

Lisa told mum that she and Emily will be going to London to join a vigil tomorrow by train. Rose was concerned about two young girls going to the big city on their own. Lisa reassured Rose that they will be alright as Emily's uncle is one of the organizers of the Vigil. He will come and pick them up from the train station once they arrive in London.

After much thought, Rose agreed to let Lisa join the Vigil, told her to phone home as soon as they arrived in London. Lisa forgot to phone home as she promised.

Next morning soon after Rose finished her morning tea, still a bit groggy after a disturbed night, she heard the doorbell ring.

"Who has come at this time?" she wondered with a dose of panic.

She heard someone knocking at the door. She stood up and slowly stepped forward. By the time she opened her door, the man had turned his back and got into a yellow van. The caller had posted an envelope through her letter box. Rose saw the yellow campervan with a damaged bumper driving away from her drive.

The letter addressed: "To Rose Edwards". She left the letter unopened on the hall table and went to find her daughter.

Lisa was not in in her room, Rose checked the bathroom, found Lisa laid on the floor, she did not respond when Rose called her name. Rose rushed to pick her daughter up, checked her breathing, noticed congealed blood on her forehead. Now she panicked, picked her mobile and phoned her next-door neighbour Ruth. John, Ruth's husband replied, "What's the matter Rose he asked, I saw a campervan in your drive when I returned from my morning walk, are you all right?"

"No, not really, I had a bad night, Lisa was in London, she came back late last night, this morning I found her unconscious on the floor of her bathroom".

"WHAT? How did it happen", asked John. Ruth, John's wife heard their conversation, said to John, "Pass me the phone, go and see Lisa, she sounds awful".

In a calm voice Ruth said to Rose, "John will be there in a minute; I shall be there soon".

Part II

By the time John arrived, Lisa opened her eyes, touched her forehead, a drop of blood smear tainted her finger.

John asked, "Lisa, how did you hurt on your head?", after a pause Lisa replied, "It was a policeman who pushed me to the ground in Clapham common last night. We were in a candle light vigil, to pay our respects to that girl who was killed, just for walking alone at night a few nights before."

Rose asked, "How did you return home? there was no train at that time?"

"Elsie's uncle gave us a lift; he is a very nice man. He asked me about my family and said he might have met you before at Manchester Uni. His name is Brian Smith. He thought you were his flatmate for a while, at that time he grew a goatee beard. Everyone used to call him Uncle Brian (after Uncle Ho Chi Min in Vietnam). We spent a lot of time talking about politics, youth rebellion, injustices, and brotherhood etc. He said that he was a born rebel, to protest and stand up against social injustices, that sort of things since he was young."

"Tell us what happened in London, how did you hurt yourself?" asked Ruth.

We went straight to Clapham Common, there were not many people to start with, later we came to know that the vigil was cancelled after the police said that this was against the law. But after a while people trickled in small numbers and we saw about three hundred gathered around the place. They were hugging and holding hands in solidarity. There was sadness and anger. By 6 o'clock hundreds gathered peacefully at the Clapham Common bandstand, bringing flowers, candles and tributes to the dead girl. The police formed a chain and began to surround the crowd. Officers handcuffed a lady, onlookers shouted, "Shame on you", one woman yelled, "You are supposed to protect us", another policeman pushed an old lady to the ground. She fell over on her knees. I was behind that lady, I was thrown against a lamp post, I got a small cut on my forehead. A young lady, saw me getting hurt, she said she was a Doctor, checked my head and my eyes. She did not think I needed to go to hospital, best advice was to avoid hospital due to the risk of Covid-19 infections.

After a while I could see a group of people singing, holding candles in their hands,

'Blowing in the Wind'
... yes, how many times must a man look up
Before he can see the Sky?
And how many ears must one man have
Before he can hear people, cry?
And how many deaths will it take 'til he knows
That too many people have died.
The answer, is blowing in the wind
The answer is blowing' in the wind my friend
Before she sleeps in the sand?

... I was so tired and exhausted when I got home, I forgot to say "Thanks" to Brian for his troubles.

When I went to the loo, I fell asleep and found myself on the floor of the toilet."

All three adults listened to Lisa in pin drop silence.

Suddenly Lisa stopped talking, she curled her lips as if she was trying to resist her cry, her eyes were misty with drops of tears, face was red with anger and fear.

Lisa said her mum, "Mum I want to visit the Cathedral tonight to light a candle for Sarah ... will you please come with me?". "Yes, I will", said Rose. She stood up and gave a hug to her daughter.

Postscript

On 30 September 2021, Lord Justice Fulford at the Old Bailey sentenced a serving police officer called Wayne Couzens to life imprisonment without parole for the kidnap, rape and murder of Sarah Everard on 3 March 2021. The judge told him:

> "During the period before your arrest, there was never a moment when you gave the slightest indication of regret, perhaps the realisation of the enormity of the dreadful crime you had committed".

Like the whole country I felt angry, hurt and sad. In my disgust I phoned my psychologist friend and asked her about psychopathic personality traits. What she told me was:

> "Study indicates the dark triad traits are a complex cluster of intertwined personality characteristics, comprised of narcissism, psychopathy and Machiavellianism. In addition,

there are a number of subdimensions recently identified regarding the smaller traits which are encompassed in this larger personality domains at subclinical psychopathy and Machiavellianism. It is possible that psychopathy is associated with more hostile parenting in higher socioeconomic households. In low socioeconomic households, there is no relationship between maternal narcissistic neurosis and hostile parenting".

Après moi le déluge

❖ ❖ ❖

In 1995 my brother Ravi enrolled at Aston University to do a Doctorate in Nuclear Physics, while his wife Priya was at the Imperial College to study Computer Sciences in London. After completing his qualifications, Ravi got a job as an Assistant Research Manager at Sellafield nuclear works. Meanwhile Priya was offered a position of Assistant Management Accountant in the City of London. Later Ravi decided to give up his job and applied for a teacher's job in a North London School.

Although Ravi and Priya are both Indians, they are from distant regions with different mother tongue, culture and traditions. However, that did not bother them as they opted to communicate in English and were deeply in love with each other.

I joined them a year later to specialise in Electrical Engineering in London. In 2002, to our pleasant surprise Priya told us that she was pregnant. The baby arrived the following year. It was a lovely eight-pound boy. I was also delighted to tell them that I was offered a job in Swindon in a car plant to design an Electric car engine. When I phoned our families in India to give the happy news, our parents were over the moon. They asked us all to visit them the following year. They were thrilled to bits and said we shall have a big party once we were there. Plan was to visit Priya's family first who lived in the town of Mahabalipuram, south east coast of India. Priya's family picked us up from the Airport and dropped us at the Hotel next to the Beach. They could not take their eyes off the little one, the first-born grandchild. As it was the Christmas day, 2004, everything looked cheerful, bright and beautiful.

Next morning on 26 December Priya's Dad said on the breakfast table that "there was a huge Tsunami in Sumatra last light. Thankfully everything here is lovely, nice and quiet." I could not see Ravi and the baby as Ravi took the baby for a walk to the beach in his pram. It was mid-morning. Suddenly we could hear a ferocious roar of rushing water, waves 20ft high. As the waves approached our hotel we noticed, everything was swept away in front of our very eyes. Priya suddenly realised her baby and husband were not there, she ran towards the sea facing the surging waters. I got on my feet like a shot and ran after her, she was hysterical, totally out of control. I managed to hold on to her with one arm bracing the concrete pillar of the porch with the other. She pulled me so strong that the pillar fell down and hit the left side of my head. I felt dizzy, confused and passed out. I could still hear Priya shouting at the wall of waters, "I am Princess Priya, daughter of Vesuvius, King of Silurian, go back, go back, this is an order". I passed out.

Suddenly like a magic, after a few minutes the maddening sea calmed down, menace waves disappeared. Priya ran to look for the baby and Ravi. Everywhere it was total chaos, people calling the names of their loved ones, a cry of surprise when some found their family, despair when they did not. They found Ravi holding on to a pillar near the beach and saw the baby's pram laid on the sand. By this time the rest of the family arrived, looking for the little boy. Priya was fighting to set free from the restrain of Ravi's arms, like a wounded she-devil losing her child. They later found the boy was at the hurricane rescue Centre, someone took him there. The shock of events made Priya loss of her voice. She did not speak a single word for a whole year and six months when she returned home to England.

After that eventful day, sometimes later, I found myself in a hospital bed. They said I was in a comma after the hit on my head by the concrete pillar. When I came around, I could hear the familiar voice of my dad talking to a man who sounded like a doctor. The doctor was telling them that I had a nasty concussion, my brain's left hemisphere seemed to have taken the blunt impact of the injury sustained. As a result, there was an impairment in my brain's circulatory in passing messages from the left hemisphere to my right hemisphere, causing my confusion."

I could hear the voice of my mum, "Will he be alright? Thanks God he is still alive". The doctor said I was a lucky man. It was not the pillar, but a flying coconut, that had knocked me out.

I was released from the hospital after ten days and returned home with my parents. I started to feel better except for the strange dreams of Priya shouting, "I am Princess Priya ... daughter of Silurian King Vesuvius".

Thinking about it, it was indeed strange that the wall of waters retreated once she ordered them to go back.

I saw a Neuropsychologist for the next three months. She said "it was quite normal to experience such dreams after such traumatic events". After a while I told her that my dreams are now less troublesome than before. She told me that it was good news, but too early to comment, it was possible that in the next stage my dreams could change. She was right, in my next lot of dreams, I saw Priya confessing to me that she was indeed a Silurian princess. Sent to earth to sabotage their arch enemy human aliens' centre of power in London Stock Exchange by infecting it with a virulent computer virus. She was a mole, sleeper cell and spy all rolled into one. Her brief was to release a virulent virus when the signal comes from the underworld.

But things did not go according to plans. She met this clever young man, my brother, fell in love head over heels, failed to accomplish the mission as planned. When the elders in the court of Vesuvius found out that one of their daughters was seduced and married to an alien, they decided to take punitive action.

The plan was to detonate a powerful explosion of unimaginable power to remind the human race that they are no more the masters of the World. It was the Silurian's turn.

Precisely at 00:58:53 UTC, on 26 December 2004, an undersea megathrust earthquake, magnitude of 9.1–9.3 was released in the Indian Ocean. On Boxing day's tsunami 230,000 people died. My brother told me (he should know, he was a nuclear scientist) that the power of the quake was equal to 23,000 Hiroshima type atomic bombs. Total damage: 15 Billion US Dollars.

Nina, my new psychologist visited me regularly for about a year. One day I told her that my dreams have changed again. She asked me to describe my dreams, to note it down on my medical records.

I told her that I saw this beautiful girl, with long black hair, a bright red bindy on her forehead between her beautiful big eyes. When she smiled at me, she was divine. She had been in my dreams every night.

Nina said, "That's excellent, its normal for a young man to have such dreams. It's a good sign. Now that your left brain has healed and communicating with the right, your brain is processing precise composite pictures of objects around."

She asked me if this girl looks like someone I knew? I nodded. Then she asked me, "Who was she like? a Bollywood film star?" I looked into her eyes and told her, "No, it was you, I saw you last night".

She stopped whatever she was doing, looked straight into my eyes for a minute, may be two, as if trying to capture every emotion and perceptions playing deep inside my mind at that particular moment of time.

She stood up and packed her bag, walked away without saying goodbye.

Next evening mum said she got an email from Nina saying that I have now fully recovered, she will not be visiting us anymore. I am now fully recovered, ready to return to work.

My mum said, "You have been footloose and fancy free for far too long. Time to settle down. Stop watching those Doctor Who episodes, you are a grown up now".

I went to my room, like a wounded teenager with a bleeding heart and wrote to Nina, "It's you, no one else who will ever fill the void in my life. I love you a lot Nina, no body but you."

Next day mum said that she had spoken to Nina's mum and both agreed that we should get married as soon as possible, may be this coming December.

Mum also said she had already spoken to Ravi and Priya. They were delighted to learn about our wedding. Ravi said they would definitely come home now that Priya's postpartum psychosis is fully recovered.

Mum said Priya told her the baby is growing up well, he can sit on his own, can creep on his hands, sometimes burst out laughing.

We got married that December.

The Bridge of Sighs

Il Ponte dei Sospiri

❖ ❖ ❖

That was an evening I still remember, clear and fresh in my memory. Sitting on a gondola sailing on the canals we marvelled at the beautiful enchanted city of Venice on a late summer day.

As we approached the Doge's Palace, we saw the fabled arched ornamental bridge, about 11-meter-long, in front of us.

There were many young couples waiting on little gondolas. All were trying to be under the bridge at the magic moment, when the sun would set and the bells would ring (at the nearby St Mark's Basilica) to kiss each other. Legend has it, that those who achieve such a feat will be blessed with everlasting love and will never be apart till the end of time.

The gondolier told us, "You know this story of everlasting love is not strictly true, it was partly the imagination of the English poet Lord Byron, who was responsible for creating the myth. It is a lovely backdrop for a photoshoot to the tourists and something to remember by of their youth and romance.

I asked him, "Was there another true story behind the myth?". He said, "Yes there was, lots of sadness surrounding this place, which the tour guides like to forget". He then told us the story. When the city was an independent city state under the rule of the Doge who was the supreme ruler. He pointed his finger to a big beautiful Palace close by. We looked at the Doge's Palace and St Mark's Basilica sitting next to the piazza which was built in honour of St Mark, whose body was buried in that Basilica.

I asked him, "Why did they call the bridge 'Bridge of Sighs'?". He told me that when they built the bridge near the harbour of the city, the fully enclosed bridge made of white lime stone was the last point where the prisoners could see the beautiful city of Venice for the very last time, before they were summarily executed during the Inquisition.

Among those notorious criminals was Giacomo Casanova who managed to escape from the terrible prisons of Doge's Palace on 25 July 1755. Although Casanova was famous for numerous illicit affairs, he also had another side to his fascinating character. Born to a show business mother and an actress, father an actor-dancer. Casanova waged a list of scams against the Europe's ruling elite.

The reputation of the bridge spread all over Europe when an English nobleman and poet, Lord Byron wrote about the city as a place of love and romance. Soon the rich and famous people of Europe and hordes of tourists from all over the planet started to visit the city.

He smiled mischievously and said, "I have not got the time to elaborate on all the antics of those two famous lotharios".

On my return home I looked up for Byron's connection to the city of Venice. In Venice he lived at Mocenigo Palace from 1816–1819 with 14 servants, 2 monkeys, a fox and two mastiff dogs. Not to mention Marianna Segati (his land lady) and a 22-year-old Margarita Cogni, his paramours while he spent winter months in Venice; both were married woman. He was flamboyant and notorious for his exploits and was a romantic, sad, guilt-ridden soul. On his return to England, he must have missed his Venetian extravaganzas.

May be his Stanza 3 reflects his thoughts:

Though the night was made for loving
And the day returns too soon
Yet we will go no more roving
By the light of the moon.

Maybe he reflected on his own sins and concluded:

"Pleasure's a sin
And sometimes
Sin's a pleasure"
... Death, so called is a thing which
Makes man weep
And yet a third of life is
Passed in sleep
The heart will break,
But broken life live on
Sorrow is knowledge is not the tree of life"
(George Gordon Byron)

Looking at the bridge across the canal in the silence of the night, he might have sighed in remorse, the reason why he called the bridge the "Bridge of Sighs".

A visit to *La Patria*

❖ ❖ ❖

An Adaptation from Ernest Hemmingway: "The cat in the rain".

Two Americans walked into the big hotel in a small-town in the south of Italy in the month of November 2020. November is usually the wettest month of the year when rainfall is around 140/600 mm in a month. On their way from the airport, they saw quaint old-fashioned villages, rugged coastline, pearl blue Ionian Sea and Rocky Mountains.

Landscapes with olive groves, small vegetable patches, wild flowers, empty roads, serene and tranquil surroundings transported them into surreal surrounds after their long and chaotic flight from New York city.

By the time of their arrival at the hotel, the place was quiet, the visitors to the close by war memorial and the surrounding gardens left to return to their homes. The taxi driver said, "It will be blizzard tonight."

They looked at the tall palm trees with silvery shadows of the last sunshine of the day. At the gate of the hotel a lone waiter looked at the couple. First, he looked at the middle-aged man, then to the younger beautiful women and thought to himself, "An odd couple, an old man with a much younger wife".

He followed the couple and helped the lady to carry her suitcase over the steps to the lobby. He said something to the old receptionist in Italian. The receptionist looked at the American and asked, "Parli Italiano? Do you speak Italian?"

The man replied, "Scusa, non ho capito (sorry, I did not understand)".

The elderly receptionist then started to speak in rudimentary English, and asked for the names of the visitors and their passports.

After checking all required documents, the receptionist allocated them a second-floor twin-bedded room with balcony and sea view. The man asked the receptionist, "a che ora è la cena?" (At what time is dinner?).

The receptionist asked, "Signore Conti, are you one of the team of Americans who will be arriving tomorrow?"

"No, I am not", said Mr. Conti, and he followed the concierge who collected their luggage and room keys. When the waiter saw the young lady he kneeled down, bent his knees held one of her hands and kissed reverentially and said something in Italian to the receptionist.

Mr Conti noticed a young man sitting at a table with his computer in the lobby. He turned his head and tried to listen to the conversation between the guest and the receptionist. He introduced himself in fluent English, "I am Marco, a reporter from Rome. I'm here to report about a group of visiting American forensic experts. They should be arriving tomorrow. They are coming to investigate and identify some human remains stolen from the nearby Military graveyards".

Mr Conti pointed his finger towards the kneeling waiter and asked the young man, "What is all this commotion about? I'm George, this is my niece Sonia, why is the waiter kneeling, what is it all about?" The reporter after speaking to the waiter said, "He thinks the girl looks like a replica of the portrait of a girl in the lounge".

"Soon the waiter bought a menu and handed it to Mr Conti. He in turn passed the menu to Sonia standing next to him. After a brief look, Sonia asked, "Have you got vegan burger for dinner?"

The receptionist said "no madam, non perdure, we only offer authentic Italian dishes in our hotel; we are open for dinner at 7.30 pm till 10 pm."

When they arrived in their room Sonia walked to the balcony. She saw the gardens and the sea. "It is still raining outside", she said to her uncle.

In the garden she saw a little cat under a table trying to avoid the driving rain and strong wind blowing from the seas.

"I'm going down to get the kitty," Sonia told her uncle.

"I'll do it", George said.

"No, I'll get it. The poor kitty is having a lot of trouble, the table is not big enough to cover her from the rain".

Uncle said, "Don't get wet, it is very windy out there tonight".

The girl went down looking for the cat, but the cat had disappeared by the time Sonia arrived where she saw the cat.

Part II. The Italian Connection

Next morning George woke up late. There was calm after the storm of the night. He looked at the other bed, Sonia was not there. Looking at his watch he noticed the time was half past nine. He looked through the widow outside and saw tables and chairs on the ground were scattered all over the yard. As he went down to the dining room, he saw the hotel owner and Sonia were chatting when the maid entered the room. They all looked gloomy and concerned. George could hear Marco's voice from the other end of the room talking on his mobile. His voice was tense and flat. The maid returned to the kitchen to bring George his breakfast.

As Marco returned to his seat he said, "Mario Draghi, Prime minister ordered lockdown from the day after tomorrow, Covid is now unstoppable. All flights to Rome are cancelled from now on". Marco looked at the hotel owner and said, "The Americans have cancelled their flights".

The owner said, "This Covid has ruined my business. No one in this town is making any money except for those grave diggers who are robbing old bones from the graves and mafia demanding extortionate money from those bereaved relatives selling them burial plots. I shall ask my staff not to come till things get better". He looked at George and said, "I think you are stuck here till we hear from the Government. He turned his head to Maria the maid and asked if she would be staying and look after the guests. Maria nodded her head and said, "I have to stay, because they cancelled the buses to my village".

After breakfast the owner looked outside and said, "I better pick up those chairs and tables and lock up the store." Marco said, "I shall come and help you". Both Sonia and George joined them to tidy up the yard to help the old man.

After they finished, Sonia and Marco went out to visit the town. George went for a walk to the beech on his own. On his return, he felt the place was deserted, silent and strange. As the day passed by, he could feel a sense of loneliness creeping in, like sadness deep down inside his heart. He thought of his only son Frank, who was in the Army, now a mental wreck after he returned from Afghanistan, they said it was PTSD. His friend Don, who used to play the piano in the arcade below his flat in New York City and the story Don told him when they became friends. Don was a musician working at the Broadway. After his wife died of cancer, Don was made redundant because of excessive drinking, lost his home, no one knew where he had gone, maybe he died of Covid like so many homeless people.

Last summer George received a phone call from Sonia his niece, telling him that she was a student at the New York University, now due to Covid everything has closed down, "Could she come and stay with him till things return to normal?" George was happy to take her in as she was her only living relative. One day George asked Sonia if she would like to visit Italy with him, from where their ancestors came from.

After couple of days, Marco decided to return to his home in Rome. As he bade farewell, he gently hugged Sonia and said "I will miss you a lot", he gave her a kiss on her lips and said, "I will never forget you, please keep in touch. I am going to tell my mamma, what a wonderful girl you are".

Maria the maid said, "Don't worry Marco, I shall mould her to be a perfect Italian wife and teach her how to cook fabulous Italian dishes like your mamma, for you and for your family."

Two weeks later Sonia left the town to be with Marco, her new found love in Rome. Handing an envelope bulging with dollars. George said to her, "This is for you my love, be happy, be blessed, take care. I shall return home soon, please keep in touch."

Maria said, "Signore Conti, she will be fine, she will be blessed by St Gertrude of Nivelles, Patron Saint of the Cats and Travellers. I shall light a candle for her safety tonight".

The thought of returning to his apartment in New York City brought the memories of being alone. A place where no one knew his name, not a familiar face, not even a phone call, no one to break the never-ending silence for days. All he would hear day after day again is an incessant piercing buzzing noise, made by the passing footsteps of strangers on the pavement.

Snippets from bygone springtime

❖ ❖ ❖

"If winter comes, can spring be far behind?" asked Shelley in his, "Ode to the West Wind".

I have seen many Springs; as Shelley noted, life is a cycle of birth and death, nature is the master of it all, we abide by the rules of nature. Spring is the time of new birth. Birth of a New year. It is the time to rejoice. Love blossoms. This is the time when earth stands between Venus the goddess of love and Mars the warrior lover. Being apart longing between the heavenly bodies intensity which spills over, lonely young hearts cry, beloved send messages –

> "Don't cry, don't cry please,
> Sun is shining, flowers blooming,
> Life's worth living now".

like the cherry blossoms, love blossoms, distance fuels desire. Soon new life replenishes our world.

In India from time immemorial arrival of the springtime is celebrated with great pomp and festivity. In my childhood I remember there was lots of music, dance, feast, and stories of love-sick youngsters eloping from the village.

Some springs monsoon rain brought floods and devastation to the community when hardship was palpable which dampened the celebration. But not the spirit.

The year I moved to Scotland, at springtime I was heartbroken missing my family, my friends, the songs, the burst of chuckle of teenaged girls, my newlywed wife. I was very home sick.

I have memories of happiness of another springtime when our daughter was born, we were young then, my wife and I brought her to our little flat, suddenly it dawned on us that we were all on our own in a foreign country. There was no one else to share our joy or the fear of the unknown, the enormous responsibility of parenthood, to advise us how to care for this delicate new life. We felt lonely, lost, helpless – we cried.

I went out of our flat, and suddenly realised we were surrounded by thousands of cherry blossoms all around us, as if to reassure us and welcome our new born daughter. I shall never forget that Spring.

The other Spring that comes to my mind is when I moved up north to a little pit village with my first proper job after years of training. It was Easter time.

The local vicar visited to welcome us. He brought us palm crosses and best wishes hoping for we shall be happy and be part of the community for years to come.

Now that the wind of autumn of my life slowly calms down my spirit, I still rejoice the songs of spring birds and the colour of spring.

August 2021

❖ ❖ ❖

Sometime in the darkness of August nights
I wake up and revisit the days of yesteryears
Last year was a year of disaster
So many friends have suffered and fallen
I must be a lucky man to be alive and well
I look at the old photos of my friends
I see their smile, my heart breaks in tears and sadness
Yesterday our grandchildren visited us
They brought happiness like a ray of sunshine
My sadness disappeared quicker than a flash
They are the reason I live and carry on
Life must go on. Destiny will decide.

On a cold winter's morning

❖ ❖ ❖

As part of my GP training, I was working at a Psychiatric hospital over the Christmas. My seniors warned me that Christmas can be a very stressful time. Over that weekend I was expected 'to hold the fort' on my own. However, as I had no family to go to, I volunteered to work that weekend. As warned, soon I was inundated with multiple calls requesting urgent admission. Although I cannot now recall the course of events, I was faced with a situation having to deal with some serious cases. The first case was a homeless lady, with post-traumatic stress disorder, strictly speaking not a mental health emergency, I did not have the heart to refuse her admission. Then there was a young girl with anorexia, very distressed, with sickness, followed by another case with suicidal idea. As the day went by more cases were admitted in the ward. The sister on call was very concerned that we ran out of beds. By the time it was 11 o'clock at night, I was completely mentally and physically exhausted. The following day was no different. I did not have time to have a shower, shave or a proper meal. I just wanted to run away to somewhere, anywhere, where I can drop off to sleep for a whole week.

Sister Jones was working that morning, she was an elderly caring traditional matron who always did her best for patients, also looked after us the trainee junior doctors like a surrogate mother, offering advice and support. Next morning when I was ready to return to my room, she suggested that instead of being on my own, maybe I should spend a few days somewhere nice, where I could chill out and relax. She knew of an Inn at Beulah which is on route A483, about an hour's drive. She said she knew the owner of the Inn and would ask him if a room was available. I agreed. I packed my bag and instead of driving, got on the bus to Beulah. Soon I dozed off. When I opened my eyes, I noted sheep pastures along the valley, winter sunshine like gold dust shining on night's sharp frost.

Next morning, I noticed that the Inn had only another guest, a young lady. I greeted her and asked her if I can join her at the breakfast table. She smiled and politely gestured to me to join her. After a lovely breakfast we chatted and talked about how we ended up in that place. She introduced herself, and told me that she was on a walking break. I told her my part of the story.

It was one of those rare winter days with sparkling sunshine, I decided to go for a walk. Trying to be polite. I asked her if she would like to join me. She said 'yes' and took leave to go to her room and got ready, she returned fully cladded in her walking gear. We went down a farm road, across the horse paddock, then the slippery hill path descending through golden oaks. I felt my stress was slowly melting away, I felt physically tired but refreshed.

Next day we went out again, high up and back down the broad green track of Beulah.

After the weekend I packed my bag and went for my breakfast. I told Amy I shall be going back by Bus. Amy said, she had nothing better to do and offered to drop me at the bus station in her car. We exchanged our mobile numbers.

About two weeks later, I got a text message from Amy, attached was a photograph, a selfie of the two of us in the valley, the scenery was so perfect that I thought it was superimposed on a set of "Frozen".

I looked at the picture a number of times, it occurred to me, maybe it was our destiny to meet each other. Another evening sitting on my own, fiddling with the TV remote control, I was thinking of Amy. I picked up my mobile and rang her. She seems to have recognised my number straight away, as if she expected my call. We chatted a long time and planned to meet up next weekend. Following week, I met her in Covent Garden. On my way I popped in a big departmental store, vaguely looking for a small gift. Suddenly a young salesman drew my attention. He was at the perfume counter. He smiled and said, "Can I help you Sir? Are you looking for something special for your lady friend?" I nodded. "In that case I can recommend you something very special". He picked out a small bottle of perfume "Issy Miyake". He sprayed a little test strip, and said, "Oh, I love it, I wear it every day", "I noticed the person had long manicured fingers and was wearing eye makeup. I asked him to gift-wrap the pack and proceeded to Covent Garden. Amy was waiting for me, wearing a beautiful Laura Ashley dress. She looked beautiful. While we were waiting for our meal, she opened the packet, squirted the perfume on her left inner wrist, and smiled.

We had a really nice time. Later I escorted her to her home. She gave me a light peck on my cheek and said goodnight. I went to the train station on my way back home.

Over a period of time, we got to know each other better and kept in contact most days. We arranged to meet up when both of us were free. I realised that she was the special person in my life. After about a year or so, I invited her to my flat. That evening I cooked a special dinner and also bought some wine. I opened a nice bottle of wine; she enjoyed the meal and later opened a bottle of Prosecco and sat down before the telly. Suddenly Amy asked me if I had a girlfriend before. I said, "yes", I told her about the girl who was my sister's pen pal from Japan on an exchange programme. "Was she beautiful", Amy asked.

I told her she was not stunning, but she had an aura of innocence about her, she was only fourteen. However, I got busy for my oncoming A level exams, my emotions had an early demise. Although I was ready for love, she was too young to know.

After a pause Amy asked, "Did you not meet anyone else since?" I said, "Yes, this time I made sure she knew my feelings".

"Why did you not tell me about her? Did you tell her you love her?" Amy asked.

I said, "Well, she never gave me a chance, she came to my flat, first she finished my bottle of wine, now she is on her second bottle of Prosecco", Amy smiled and poured the left-over bottle of Prosecco on my head. In fact, I was so nervous that I probably drank most of it.

I knelt down and asked, "Amy will you marry me?"

She looked serious and quietly said, "Of course I will"

I opened the little box and put the ring in her ring finger.

She gave me a wet kiss. Then she said, "I am really cross with you; I did not even bring a nice dress to celebrate the occasion.

We opened a bottle of Champagne sat in the cooler. We decided to get married the following springtime.

The realities of life

I dropped Amy at the train station and returned to my flat after we got engaged the night before. There were unwashed mugs on the coffee table, one with smudged lipstick, I went to the bathroom, Amy's perfume was still smelling strong, she forgot her eye brow pencil. Suddenly on reflection, that we are now betrothed, I panicked, I have not as yet found a job, no home, no security. Have not told my parents, will she get on with my family? I collapsed on the sofa.

When I got an interview from a practice in Matlock in Derbyshire, she loved the place. We lived in a cute little cottage near the town. The steep hills and sounds of the flowing river, the parks, fresh mountain air, made us feel welcome. Both senior doctors were polite and welcoming.

Following spring we got married at the local church, followed by a Hindu ceremony. It was a quaint affair.

Soon I got busy, Amy became a full-time housewife. At times she missed her family and friends and busy London life. One day she told me, "You know, no one calls me by name here, I am only the doctor's wife".

She still tried to fill her time reading books, going to the mountains for long walks. But that was not enough to fill her time. We decided to start a family.

We were blessed with a little girl.

I became very busy, as both my seniors decided to cut down their work load in preparation to retirement. We were informed that all practices would be updated and computerised. My seniors did not want to get involved. Both of them retired the following January. I became the doctor responsible for modernization. My work increased tenfold. I hardly had any time to play with my little girl, Amy found it hard to cope with a new baby alone, caring for the family, shopping, cooking, as my unpaid secretary, answering the phone all God-given hours, trying to deal with a haggard ill-tempered husband. We decided to have another child so that Lily our daughter would have someone to grow up with. In due course a second bundle of love arrived, a boy. Now we were a complete family.

We moved to a much bigger house. I had to take on more jobs to meet the additional costs. As there was a huge shortage of doctors, pressure of work increased even more. Amy too found it hard to cope. One Friday, I promised to return home early to take the family out. I was held up at the surgery with a very ill man. By the time I arrived home it was too late.

We had a flaming row, Amy said that I had changed from being a kind husband, a good dad to a work crazy monster.

Despite, my attempts to pacify her; Amy was not convinced. She stormed out of the room. Kids were woken up from their sleep. When I went upstairs both of them got out of their beds and were peeping through the crack of the door, frightened with tears on their eyes. I picked them up, took them to their beds and tried to hum a lullaby.

Next morning, I rang my GP friend Tony and told him I was in trouble. We arranged to meet up at the Red Lion at lunch time. Tony understood, he said, I was suffering from burn out like half the GP population in the country. Many of them are considering early retirement. He said, to take some time off, go back to a part time work before it is too late. He said, it was the pressure how he lost his wife.

Sometime in between our parents passed away, I went through a period of depression.

There were some happy times in between, I received a letter from New York University informing me that I shall be able to peruse my research on my special interest in their laboratories for a period of three months during the summer holidays. We decided to go to America as a family trip. We had a great time, now my research work was nearly complete.

Time went by, kids grew up fast, they went to their chosen universities, we missed them a lot, suffered from empty nest syndrome. Amy missed them the most.

We have grown old. Last week I apologised to Amy for the things that I did wrong.

She said that I stopped loving her a long time ago, she knew I did care, never short of anything all these years ... now she is all alone." Tears rolled down her face, she cried.

I wondered, is love an illusion at the end of a rainbow or a prelude to delusions of realities of life.

The Future Ahead
I still meet Tony from time to time. He also took early retirement and bought a villa in Spain. Last weekend he visited us to wish me "A happy birthday".

He brought a CD sang by Toby Keith for his friend Clint Eastwood. Don't let the old man in.

> "Many moons I lived
> My body is weathered and worn
> Ask yourself how old you'd be
> If you did not know the day you were born
>
> Try to love your wife
> And stay close to your friends
> Toast each sundown with win
> Don't let the old man in."

Dinner with my uncle

❖ ❖ ❖

It was an autumn evening; I think in mid-October in the year 1950. My uncle asked me to keep him company while he decided to buy a new sports jacket.

He dressed up in his dark blue suit with a blue tie, with a matching hat and a handkerchief in his chest pocket. He wore a pair of dark brown shoes which he would wear only for important events. He carefully filled his golden cigarette box with his Player's Medium brand cigarettes. Then he opened his golden Ronson gas lighter to check if the sparkling ignition was in working order. Although I was a bit bemused by his sudden burst of favours to me I was very happy to visit the city with my favourite uncle.

We went to Regent Street for our dinner, the restaurant had an Indian name, I think it was called Veeraswami Indian Restaurant. The whole area was packed with people.

I saw most men were dressed in smart suit and ladies were dressed in formal skirts and blouses. The waiters looked very smart in their long aprons with waistcoats and jackets. They were very busy serving the people sitting and chatting and laughing with cans of Double Diamond beers. Women were drinking Pina Colada. Soon a young lady approached our table, my uncle looked very happy and attentive to her and called her to our table.

He introduced me to the lady and said, "This is my nephew. Yes, he is the one who joined Westminster School last year, I bought him to meet you as he is the only relative, I have in

London. He then introduced the lady and said, "Here is my friend Tracey, she has agreed to marry me and you can call her aunty Tracey.

After a while the waiter brought us a menu to order our food. The list included many items, some of the names were unfamiliar to me and I did not know what they were. I saw the names like Mulligatawny soup, fish rissoles, kedgeree, chutney but decided to order roti and sabji ice cream.

My uncle explained the menu to his friend Tracey and they ordered their chosen dishes. After they ordered their food, my uncle ordered a bottle of Champagne and another bottle of wine.

Tracey raised her glass of champagne, so did my uncle. He asked me to fill my glass with water and we all raised our glasses saying "Cheers".

I really enjoyed my ice-cream which was the best I have ever had, I looked at my uncle who was a very relaxed. By now my uncle became a bit too friendly, he stood up and said "Cheers", he then gave a kiss to Tracey, they hugged each other and enjoyed the day full of love and joy. I asked my uncle if I can have another ice-cream, he said, "Yes, the world is your oyster". I said to him, "No uncle I don't want an oyster, all I want is another big Cornetto ice cream.

A letter to my parents

❖ ❖ ❖

Dear Mum and Dad

5 August 1977

Hope you all are doing well. You asked me how we spend our summer holiday in England. Last week we visited Whitby a local seaside town and thought of sending a photograph from the boat house where we stayed the night.

My first visit to English seaside

We live in a little mining town called Worksop. Recently I joined the local Lion's Club. The club owns a small seaside cabin at Whitby which offers short holiday break to ill and elderly people. I volunteered to take an elderly couple and their disabled son to that cabin last weekend.

On my way we had long chats when I learned about their life and how they used to earn a living in the olden days. The man said he used to be in the East Yorkshire Regiment during the second world war when he was in his twenties. He was sent to fight in Normandy on the first day of the Allied invasion of Nazi occupied Europe. His wife said her family lived in a mining village near Worksop, father was a miner near Firbeck colliery at that time. Her dad died in an accident when the roof of the mine collapsed few years ago. Her husband John asked me, "Where are you from?", I said, "From India".

Their son Mathew said, "You speak like Peter sellers in the film *The Millionairess*, then he smiled and stated to sing: "Goodness

Gracious Me ... boom bloody boom-boom, bloody-boomboom". On the whole I enjoyed chatting with all three of them. I asked John how did he meet Elsie his wife?

John said, he met Elsie when he visited his uncle in her village. They fell in love at the first sight and decided to get married soon after their first date. After they got married Elsie's mum gave a one-pound note to Elsie to visit Whitby for their honeymoon. It was a very windy day, when she opened her purse, the note flew off her fingers. John chased the note but could not retrieve her money. So, the newlywed couple could not visit Whitby on that occasion. After the war they visited the town many a times where their son was conceived. The couple laughed out loud talking about their fiasco of that day. John said he still remembers his old colleagues who died at Normandy, all twenty-two of them, it was 6 June 1944.

Once we arrived at Whitby, we went to the seaside. John pointed his finger to an old red brick house and said, "This is Captain Cook's museum. Captain Cook used to work at Whitby ship company. One day, he jumped ship and joined the Royal Navy. Later he circumnavigated the world from New Zealand and east coast of Australia, subdued the natives, looked for the Bering Strait. When he arrived in Hawaii, he was killed by the Hawaiian Islanders and his bones were removed. They believed the power of a man was in his bones so they cooked his body to remove his bones. There is a statue in memory of captain Cook at Whitby."

Next, we visited Whitby Abbey overlooking the North Sea. The place is famous for stories about Dracula and ghosts and myths about supernatural events. There are many other tales of horrors associated with that god-forsaken haunted place.

We walked along the seafront where we saw the Fish and Chip shops at quayside where people lined up for hours. I bought ice-creams for all of us as it was a hot day and waited for our table. After a while we found a table and enjoyed our lovely Fish and Chip dinner.

By now the sun was setting, spraying the last glare of the splendour of the day. I dropped my charges in their cabin and stayed the night at the Boat house near the sea.

Although we were strangers till that morning, meeting them made me feel as if we were one family by the end of the day.

A cruise holiday with my family

❖ ❖ ❖

On 26 July 2019, me and my family arrived in Barcelona to join the cruise ship "Bellissima" to celebrate the big birthday of my wife. Around the time we boarded the ship, the sun was setting across the sea into the golden hour of the day. Our granddaughters were excited, dazed in utter amazement when we finally embarked into the ship. Soon we arrived on the deck of our allotted cabins. From our balcony I saw the setting sun painting a psychedelic multi-coloured canvas spread across the sky as if to welcome us on-board the ship. I could smell the stale waft of diesel from many small pilot boats. Sound of horns of departing vessels, voices of locals talking from the galleys, farewell wishes from friends and relatives waving from the mooring site. The place was buzzing with activities all around.

In the horizon, the last glimmer of sunshine gradually disappeared and replaced by reflexions of electric lights and man-made glitters on the waters. The sea now turned grey and dull losing the glorious beauty of scattered sunshine created by the last glare of the day.

Next morning my wife and I went for our morning walk to the top floor deck and watched the rising sun when the ship was manoeuvred out the harbour by the pilot boats. The route to sail along was via Costa Brava. As we approached southern Italy, we saw the town Cabo San Sebastiano visible from the portside basking in the morning sun. After a short journey we heard the

PA system announcing that we had now entered into the Gulf of Lion which was diagonally on the North-Eastern route until we arrived in the Gulf of Marseille and would then dock at the cruise terminal. We then proceeded to the top floor restaurant waiting for the rest of the family to join us. There was a huge display of food to suit everyone's taste buds, offering delicacies from Japan to Mexico, and long queues of hungry passengers. The aroma of international cuisines of all description invaded our nostrils and we ended up with too many items on our plates.

After our breakfast my wife and I went to explore different floors of the ship when the ship passed through the Italian border and we saw the cities like San Remo, Imperia and Savona from our starboard side on our way to Genoa. I remember the elegant buildings, the hillocks and valleys of the old city and the faraway olive groves shimmering under the hot sun. I recalled my previous visit to Italy when we visited an olive grove and saw the delicate foliage, twisted trunks and the smell of dry heat emitted by those old olive trees. It brought back memories of the old city we visited, like a time capsule of long gone past, still bright and beautiful and an exciting amazing place.

Next day we went to visit the Cathedral of San Lorenzo when the sun was shining through the ancient window magnifying the grace and beauty created by nature and human ingenuity and love of God. The sun was moving towards the west with linear spray of soft sunshine bringing in a sense of beauty, serenity and divinity and peace.

Next stop was Valletta in Malta. We arrived at Valletta from Messina at 8am, following the route via the Sicilian coast, Ionian Sea and finally arrived in Malta in the early hours of the morning. We had a whole day to spend in the town. It was a very hot day.

Our guide told us that according to legend the temptress nymph Calypso lured Odysseus to Gozo. She kept him as a prisoner for seven long years captivated by her beauty and charm. These days Valletta is a place of destination for tourists lured by the glimmering red sand of Ramia Bay, tranquil warm pools and gaiety of the locals. We enjoyed our day at Valletta sitting on the sand till the sunshine mellowed when our day trip ended.

That night we had a party in one of the restaurants of the ship, the staff were briefed about my wife's surprise birthday celebration in advance. The Filipino head waiter was very helpful, like a friend as our grandchildren treated him like a family member. He organised special treat with balloons, buntings and a band played music to celebrate grandma's birthday in pomp and style. Our grandchildren were so moved by the gesture of the head waiter, all three hugged him in great affection.

We noticed Josh the waiter was overwhelmed by their gesture; his eyes were filled with tears. He said those three little girls reminded him of his own daughters, he had not seen for the last nine months.

Next morning, we sailed to Barcelona on our return journey home. We found Josh at the jetty waiting to say goodbye to us. I asked him "is everything okay at home, did you ring your family last night?" He said, "Yes, I told my wife about you and your family and told her about your beautiful girls". My wife said, "Josh, I know you are missing your family, I am sure they too are missing you every minute of the day and night".

"Yes, I know Josh replied, Angel and Mimi, they have gone to bed now", they said, "Dad we all love you, come back home soon, granddad has gone out fishing tonight just after the sun set. Forecast is that there is a storm brewing, we hope he will be safe".

Josh looked at his watch and said, "At this time of the year typhoon lashes the island where my family live, it is on the edge of the Pacific ring of fire. Last year when dad and my uncle went out fishing one night, a typhoon lashed out, they were lucky to get back home alive. At daybreak when the sun was shining, the villagers gathered their belongings of what was left, struggling to survive another dismal hard day ahead".

Sylvia[*]

❖ ❖ ❖

I was young and free like a butterfly in the spring of my life
I dreamt of happiness, joy and fun.
When I fell in love, all I wanted was a little nest
Blessed with two little toddlers cuddly and sweet
Soon I realized that my dreams are chained with inherited padlocks
Innocently passed on in genes, because they had no other options.
"Freedom" is a word of illusion to human
"Success" is reaffirmation of parental personal expectations.
Every young heart carries the burden of debt passed on from father to the child
Unable to erase the markings ingrained in the deep dark caves of our minds
Etherealities of life are full of lies,
The bondage of everlasting paternal love
Is full of shites.
The curse of my birth I was destined to bear
Ecstatic moments followed by fear
My soul is relentlessly tormented by despair
Goodbye my friends, the dual conflicts of joyous positivity and despair
I can't shake off my mind.

---

[*]A Tribute to Sylvia Plath (1932–1963)

auld lang ayne

❖ ❖ ❖

On the last day of the year, we celebrated the end of another decade. We talked about yesterycars, we laughed and joked, revisited the memories of bygone days, forgotten times and of old acquaintances. We offered our hands to our trusted friends and another toast of good will drink for the year ahead.

I thought I shall write down the memories of yesteryears, however with fading memory, words get jumbled up, faces too. Only the tune and fragments of old songs cling on somewhere deep in my mind.

Like Ann Hatchway's song "There was a time when men were kind, voices were soft, words were inviting and love was blind. I was young and unafraid".

One New Year's Eve many moons ago, I met a girl, never seen anyone so lovely as she did that night.

When she turned to me and smiled, it took my breath away and I knew I have fallen in love not to be apart for the rest of my life.

I dreamt of a brave new world, "Where there is no country, Nothing to kill or die for. Living life in peace, hoping the world will be heaven one day".

I became a dreamer too. I believe as Churchill said, "Making a living by what we get, but we make a life by what we give".

In the autumn of my life, I, too would like to join Frank Sinatra and sing the song:

"I've lived a life that's full
I travelled each and every way
And more, much more then this
I did it my way".

Déjà vu of a cobbled street

❖ ❖ ❖

A few years ago, one of my friends from India asked me to book a room for him in a central London hostel as he was planning to train as a barrister at the Honourable Society of Inner Temple. Ideally, he wanted to be close to his college. As he was on a student's bursary, he was looking for cheap accommodation. After I made some enquires, I found out that the Indian YMCA hostel at Fitzroy Square suited his bill and booked a room for him.

The day after he arrived, I went to meet him and to look around the place. I bought a local map and we went ahead to explore the locality on foot. We were amazed to find out that the hostel is surrounded by classical buildings, next to the famous BT tower, art galleries, lovely cafes, West-end theatres, abuzz with activities, where history and modernity cohabitate side by side. We were surprised to find that there were many narrow alleyways connecting Charlotte Street in Fitzrovia as if a traditional small shire village is encased in a time capsule in the busiest city of the world.

Even today when I see a cobble stone alleyway, Fitzrovia's memories pass through my mind, home of worthies like Virginia Woolf, Bertrand Russell, Thomas Dylan and Charles Dickens.

But for many centuries that area was the home of London's poorest citizens known for abject poverty when narrow blind alleys and passages were lined with squalid dwellings for the lowest class of criminals, labourers and loafers. This was the place where Charles Dickens got the inspiration to write *The Pickwick papers*.

Charles Booth recorded the miseries of those wretched people:

> "The worst social conditions – both moral as well as physical – were linked directly to actual plan and gain of a district. Blind streets, yards, and alleys approached via a single entrance tended to harbour the worst extremes of deprivation and crime. Some of these can be seen here – Dickensian warrens of sunless courts and alleys; houses cheek by jowl with toxic industries, melancholy streets caked in a penitential grab of soot, ... squalid houses in poignant groups."

Captain Thomas Coram, a retired sea Captain philanthropist noted that the streets of London were littered with abandoned malnourished children, homeless families, ill and infirm old people, whereas the rich and greedy squandered their money and privileges in debauchery and decadence. After his retirement he initiated a project to establish a hospital for all destitute children he found in the streets of London with the support of Lord Salisbury, William Hogarth and George Frederic Hendel the composer. They named the hospital as Foundling Hospital. This was the first children's charity in United Kingdom. The hospital continues today as the children's charity Coram.

A warren of sunless courts
In 1902 Charles Booth revealed that the highest concentration of poverty in London – 68 per cent – could be found in the area between Blackfriars and London Bridge, poisoned by toxic fumes from nearby white lead, gas and engineering works, the squalid maze of dingy streets and sunless alleys behind Bankside contained some of the worst housing in London.

> "The surrounding streets are mean and close; poverty and debauchery lie festering in the crowded alleys, an air of gloom and dreariness seems to hang about the scene, and to impart to it a squalid and sickly hue."
> (Charles Dickens, *The Pickwick papers*).

White Hind Alley was a narrow passage lined on one side by mean dwellings and on the other by a high wall to a timber yard which blocked out the light to the houses.

Parts of Moss's Alley were less than 8ft wide, but provided access to a whole nest of small subsidiary courts and yards crammed with families categorised by Booth in the lowest class as semi-criminal, along with occasional labourers and loafers, their children classified as street "Arabs".
(Philip Davies, *Lost London 1870–1944*)

A place called home

❖ ❖ ❖

Many years ago, after the birth of our son, we were toying with the idea of buying a more spacious house to accommodate our growing family.

One day we went out to look around the town we lived in, just to find out a suitable house that fitted my budget and met my wife's expectations. We saw an old house in a secluded cul-de-sac, a bay-fronted Edwardian red brick house. While we stopped our car, an old man approached us and said that he was the owner and that the house was for sale. I noticed my wife was excited and eager to look inside the house. The old man invited us to his house. As we walked through the drive, we noticed beautiful roses in the front garden. The property appeared to be neglected, as if crying out for tender loving care to bring back its lost charm and beauty and glory of a bygone time. The owner took us to the back door of his house and said he lived alone and would like to move to a bungalow as the house was too big for him. As we walked inside the kitchen, we noticed piles of dirty dishes, peeling wall papers, water stain on the high ceiling. The huge kitchen 20x15 ft. attached to a larder where he hanged his meat from the ceiling, there was no freezer.

We saw a tatty old carpet in his lounge and layers of dust all over the place. It was a warm day, but we could smell the damp and feel the chill in each and every room we visited. In his bedroom there were a set of lovely mahogany furniture including a bedstead and cupboards. The old man said, since his divorce, he seldom used the upstairs rooms. All upstairs bedrooms were big, filled with stale mouldy damp musty smell.

Then we went to look at the back garden, there were lots of fruit trees and a huge greenhouse leaning against the back-brick wall with overgrown vegetation. Outhouses and staff toilets and the garage were full of stuff waiting for disposal for many years.

On our return home, I did not feel a welcoming feeling to that place, but my wife said she liked the house and said once renovated this will be beautiful place for us to set up a home, a secure nest to bring up our little family.

Over a period of time I mellowed, in my mind I could conceive my wife's creative insights.

Finally, we bought the creaky old house.

We renovated and refurbished the house to its original glory. I started to attend local auction houses to acquire suitable period furniture to match the ambience of the place.

Painted the front door in dark green colour, cleaned up the patterned tile floor in the hallway, placed a grandfather clock, a cut-glass chandelier in the hall ceiling, and an oak hall stand to rest our hats.

Lounge was furnished with a three-piece Chesterfield suit and matching coffee table, chairs, an old Piano for our daughter, walls adorned by two large oil paintings, one on top of the Henley and Kingston Marble Fire place.

The dining room was filled with a 12ft long telescopic mahogany table with eight matching dining chairs, a limited-edition large painting up on the wall. Also a few pieces of Belgium tapestry to compliment the surroundings.

But we had to modernise our bathrooms. Kitchen and central heating. By the time we completed all renovations, thirty years had passed by. By then our children Grew up.

Soon they left for university, found jobs, met their partners and in due course they got married. We missed our children a lot, by now they were no longer only our children, now they became responsible adults ... a time for transition, feelings of loneliness, sadness. There was no one to play the piano, no more the strumming sounds of our son's guitar. We felt the emptiness echoing all over in our empty house. A sense of that lasted a whole year. The house felt like a pile of red bricks, an empty shelter, as if it lost its soul for ever ... no more a Home, just another building like any other.

In my mind,

> "I hope, when our children are grown, they will still come through the front door without knocking. I hope they will head to the kitchen for a snack, and slump on a sofa to watch TV. I hope they will come in and feel the weight of adulthood leave them, for they are at Home. For my children ... my door will be open forever."
>
> (Author Unknown).

My Ergo chair

❖ ❖ ❖

Looking back, since I completed my qualifications there had been a revolution on how to make my posterior comfortable. In my college days all classrooms were furnished with solid wooden benches behind a desk fixed to the floor. In those cramped lecture rooms, I preferred to sit on a back raw to avoid my teacher's attention in case he would point his finger at me to ask me a question or in case he would find me dozing away in boredom.

After I graduated, as a junior I was able to sit on a padded chair while doing my job. As I progressed up the ladder my sitting arrangements improved over the time. Now I was eligible to sit on a well-padded swivel chair. As and when I became a senior my chair changed again, finally I earned my status when a leather covered chair with castors was provided to me so that I could easily reach for things without having to get on my feet.

Over the years I developed a liking for my old chair, softened by time, flattened by my weight, creaking in joints.

By then Computers became part of everyday life and my office manager after attending a "Safety at work" meeting came back and reported that all old chairs must be retired. Because the old-style office chairs were considered to be unacceptable as they tend to tip over and throwing off the occupant on the floor.

Next step was to get some Ergonomic office chair, designed by a German, Wilfred Dauphin. He was asked to investigate the effect of computer on furniture in office. Now we got adjustable seats, armrests, backs, back supports and heights to prevent repetitive stress injuries and back pain.

I am sure, although human anatomy has not changed in many millenniums, our zeal for comfort will pave new ideas to maximise our comforts.

A virtual reunion of batch 1962

❖ ❖ ❖

Last weekend we had a virtual reunion of my batch of entrants to Assam Medical College in India.

The convener sent me an email informing me that the meet was due to start at 6.30 pm Indian standard time. I was indeed excited with the prospect of meeting my old friends after five decades.

However, there was a technical hitch. the video pictures were grainy and, I could see faces of a group of old people in different frames sitting in the lounge of their homes. It was not ideal but they made me happy just hearing their voices and trying to put a name to their faces.

Three of them briefly saw my face and shouted in unison, "Can you recognise me Utpal?" Someone said, "You have not changed a bit after all these years".

I knew they were fibbing … so was I.

Soon the convener declared the function as officially open, and that followed playing of our college anthem. There was a brief time of silence till the anthem came to an end. We all tried to remember the words of that song, but I only recalled the tune, not even a word. That followed a round of discussion, who was the composer and who wrote the lyrics, we tried to rewind our memories of our youth and faces of our teachers propped up in our memories of a bygone time. The song defiantly changed our moods, we could feel the shadows of nostalgia creeping in from long gone past.

Our convener looked at the day's agenda, and said "Item 3: Let us now pay our respects to all our colleagues who have passed away since we left Assam Medical college".

He then sombrely read a long list of names of all those friends who have passed away.

I looked at the list, one-third of our group were in that list.

People who were in my wish list for a visit on next opportunity have died ... a sobering thought passed through our minds. Someone started sobbing in her room, I could feel the impact of such unexpected deaths among the participants.

We chatted about our family, work and life. We joked about the follies of our youth, lamented for the missed opportunity of sharing the joy and excitement meeting together, a time of our youth full of dreams like a rainbow, our dreams of a perfect world.

After the meeting I sat on my own in my lounge and thoughts of our youth ... memories of my friends flooded-in in my mind, it was a long time ago, but I still treasure their friendship, lifelong bondage forged together never fell apart.

Today while I wrote this story, with my aching heart, I told myself "I am a lucky man, I had so many friends with a golden heart, together we all tried our best to make our Alma mater proud of us."

Thanks for the privilege.

I received an email from my American friend. She wrote:

> "I was just wondering why this entire World seems to be under a cloud of constant misery. Why we all seem to be like Russians waiting in line for toilet paper, meat, Lysol, hoarding yeast and sourdough starter, in case we can't get bread".

My mind took to its wings when,

> "Clouds come flooding into
> My life, no longer to carry rain or usher a storm
> But to add colour to my sunset sky"
>
> (Tagore)

Regrets, yes, I have a few and remorse,
For failing to meet my friends
Who are here no more,
There is guilt embedded deep in my heart
because I knew, we all were on borrowed time.

Like a kite, my windswept mind thought of Frank Sinatra and I sang a little song –

> "I've lived a life that's full
> I travelled each and every way
> And more, much more then
> this I did it my way".

Goodbye my sweetheart

❖ ❖ ❖

The caretaker was waiting for Johnny to finish the last song for the night.

It was the party to end all parties. They had fun, they danced, they drank like there was no tomorrow, they had hugged and sang all night. By the time Johnny finished everyone but the caretaker gone home. When the lights went off, there was no one to encore. He felt let down, once he and his band were very much in demand, the thrill of knowing that the audience enjoyed and cheered for an encore. Those days may never come back again. All they had tonight, was an illegal rave. They broke all the rules of social distancing that night.

This year everything changed. The roar of 210 000 did not happen. Taylor Swift, Sir McCartney, Stormzy and the likes of him never happened. Last year at this time gates were open at 8 am, buzz of excitement of pitching up tents, running around spreading the happiness of rites of passage. Now all this is memory of bygone generations.

It is a sad tale after fifty years of celebration.

This is not the end, there will be a new beginning in the horizon.

I know you are missing the fun, there will be another Glastonbury come rain or shine.

Goodbye my sweetheart till next time.

Printed in Great Britain
by Amazon